HER RIVAL COWBOY

BROTHERS OF MILLER RANCH BOOK THREE

NATALIE DEAN

OTHER BOOKS BY NATALIE DEAN

CONTEMPORARY ROMANCE

Miller Family Saga

BROTHERS OF MILLER RANCH

Miller Family Saga Series 1

Her Second Chance Cowboy

Saving Her Cowboy

Her Rival Cowboy

Her Fake-Fiance Cowboy Protector

Taming Her Cowboy Billionaire

Brothers of Miller Ranch Complete Collection

MILLER BROTHERS OF TEXAS

Miller Family Saga Series 2

The New Cowboy at Miller Ranch Prologue

Humbling Her Cowboy

In Debt to the Cowboy

The Cowboy Falls for the Veterinarian

Almost Fired by the Cowboy

Faking a Date with Her Cowboy Boss

Miller Brothers of Texas Complete Collection

BRIDES OF MILLER RANCH, N.M.

Miller Family Saga Series 3

Cowgirl Fallin' for the Single Dad

Cowgirl Fallin' for the Ranch Hand

Cowgirl Fallin' for the Neighbor

Cowgirl Fallin' for the Miller Brother

Cowgirl Fallin' for Her Best Friend's Brother

Cowboy Fallin' in Love Again

Brides of Miller Ranch Complete Collection

Miller Family Wrap-up Story

(An update on all your favorite characters!)

Copper Creek Romances

<u>BAKER BROTHERS OF COPPER CREEK</u>

Copper Creek Romances Series 1

Cowboys & Protective Ways

Cowboys & Crushes

Cowboys & Christmas Kisses

Cowboys & Broken Hearts

Cowboys & Second Chances

Cowboys & Wedding Woes

Cowboys' Mom Finds Love

Baker Brothers of Copper Creek Complete Collection

<u>CALLAHANS OF COPPER CREEK</u>

Copper Creek Romances Series 2

Making a Cowgirl

Marrying a Cowgirl

Christmas with a Cowgirl

Trusting a Cowgirl

Dating a Cowgirl

Catching a Cowgirl

Loving a Cowgirl

Marrying a Cowboy

Callahans of Copper Creek Complete Collection

KEAGANS OF COPPER CREEK

Copper Creek Romances Series 3

Some Cowboys are Off-Limits

Some Cowgirls Love Single Dads

Some Cowboys are Infuriating

Some Cowboys Don't Like City Girls

Some Cowboys Heal Broken Hearts

Some Cowboys are Just Friends (Coming July 2024)

Though I try to keep this list updated in each book, you may also visit my website nataliedeanauthor.com for the most up to date information on my book list.

CONTENTS

1

———

Danielle

$\mathcal{A}$ terrifying, splintering sound roused Danielle from her sleep. She blinked blearily, rolling onto her side to turn on the lamp by her bed, only to realize that her room was far more illuminated than it had any right to be in the dead of night.

Red, orange, and yellow flickered across her vision, almost pretty until she realized exactly what those colors meant.

"FIRE!"

She vaulted out of bed, grabbing the dressing robe hanging nearby and throwing open her bedroom door.

"Fire!" she cried, running to her brothers' room and banging as hard as she could. She didn't even wait to see if they heard; she was off and racing to her parents' master bedroom.

More pounding on the door. It wasn't like Danielle had much of a plan or any idea what to do. All she knew was that there was *something* on fire, and if she could see it from the window of her second-story room, then it was something *big*.

"What? Dani, what did you say?" came Papa's groggy voice through the door.

"Call the fire department!" she said before rushing down the stairs.

Dani had never been much for speed. She could plod on forever, her dogged determination rarely ever running out, but she wasn't who one would look to for a sprint.

But she was sprinting then, flying out the door and to the side of the house where their two biggest barns were.

Were being the key word. Because where there had once been two pretty buildings, all she saw were flames.

"The animals!" she cried, rushing forward. In the back of her mind perhaps she knew that running *toward* a fire was crazy, but how could she leave living creatures to burn?

While her family's setup was no Miller Ranch, whose whole advertising was how happy and well-treated their animals were, the Touheys had also rejected the cruel, merciless strategies of modern livestock. Of course, that meant they had to keep themselves small-scale until they were able to build more of a brand. As only a second-generation ranch family, that brand had a long way to go.

Although currently, the brand was going up in flames in front of her.

She reached the doors and quickly flipped the small wooden latch that kept it closed. It was hot to the touch and she let out a yelp, yanking her hand away.

The pain, however, was quickly forgotten as she heard the panicked screams and yelps from inside. There were few things worse than the sound of a terrified, trapped animal, and what she was hearing was multiplied tenfold.

Grabbing the bottom of her old sleep shirt and ripping as hard as she could, she managed to tear off a thick strip. She wrapped it around her still-smarting hand and tried again.

This time she managed to keep her grip and finished shoving the latch upward before yanking the door open. Smoke billowed out in a thick cloud, and she barely had time to catch the sound of hooves thundering toward her before the door burst the rest of the way open and several horses came charging out.

Dani dove to the side, toppling over a bench as the normally graceful and friendly animals peeled out like speed demons. She wished they would stop, so she could check their wounds and whisper comforting things to them, but she knew there wasn't a chance that would happen.

She stumbled to her feet, panting, but not nearly enough animals raced by. While her family wasn't wealthy enough to have more than a horse each, they did offer a service where they housed and stabled the horses of rich folk from the city. Although they were insured, Dani couldn't imagine having to tell anyone that their beloved animal had perished in one of the most painful ways to go.

Pulling the fabric from her hand, she tied it around her nose and mouth. Rushing forward again, she stumbled through the smoke.

It was hot, so hot, and *loud.* Why had no one ever taught her how loud a fire was? The flames surged around her, crackling as they hungrily devoured what they could. Violent little fingers of scarlet and viridian, they greedily tried to consume everything.

There, in the back, she heard panicked whinnying and bleating. That was where they kept the smaller, shyer horses who preferred the quiet, and the goats.

The *goats!*

While the Touhey Ranch had all the classic staples, their real income bringer, what their whole brand was based on, was their happy little goats.

There were the videos online of them playing about and vaulting off the various structures her brothers had built for them out of extra items from around the ranch. There was also the goat cheese, the goat milk. Even goat milk soap! Last year her parents had managed to land a distributing contract with a small chain of organic stores, and the profit from that had significantly helped them pay down almost all of their debts.

She knew all of those goats as if they were family dogs, and she could hear them bleating in a blind panic. So, she pushed through the heat and haze, smelling so many things burning that it was making her nauseous. Was that her hair? It seemed like it might be her hair.

"Here guys!" she called before pulling her mask down to purse her lips into a whistle. "Can you hear me? This way!"

A whinny sounded to her right so she lurched that way, using her robe to cover her hand as she felt for the latch of the stall. She heard the distinctive sizzle of skin but kept going. She had to keep going.

She threw the door open and moved to the side as the panicked horse fled out. That fueled her further, allowing her to go to the next stall. And then the next.

Dani was dizzy, oh so dizzy, and it felt like her lungs were being abraded with sandpaper. Her footsteps faltered, and she tried to catch herself on a bench only to land into a smoldering pile of hay.

Yelping, she forced herself up to her feet. She could still hear the goats bleating. Where were they? Shouldn't she have reached their pen by now? When had the barn grown so long? And why couldn't she *stand*?

Her eyes were watering, her mind was spinning, and everything was a mess. It was hot. So *hot*! And she couldn't breathe.

"Dani!"

Vaguely she heard a sound at the edge of her mind and then strong hands were gripping her. She tried to look back at who was hauling her to her feet and pulling her out, but everything was so dark. Cloaked in ash and misery.

And then, suddenly, it wasn't blazing hot anymore, and her makeshift mask was being ripped from her face. She inhaled a deep breath of cool, cleansing night air only to dissolve into a coughing fit.

"The goats!" she cried between hacks. "They're trapped in there. I don't know how."

"It's okay, Dani."

That sounded like Chester. Was it Chester? She couldn't tell. It felt like her ears were stuffed with cotton and her insides were on fire. But she was out of the inferno, right?

"It's not okay!" she heaved. "We can't just let them burn alive. It's not right."

The sound of footsteps. Several sets. She looked up, but she could only see hazy outlines, her eyes feeling as if she had rubbed glass into them.

"James, get the hose from the side of the house. Turn it on full blast."

"I don't think that a garden hose is going to do much to—"

"It's not for the fire, it's for *us*. Now go!"

Dani saw the slightly smaller form run off. He seemed to return almost too quickly, hose in his hand going at full blast.

"Soak us," Chester said with authority.

The middle child of their little trio did so, turning the hose on Chester and then himself. Both of them seemed to be moving at an impossible speed, jumping jerkily from one movement to the next, or maybe that was just what her damaged eyes and foggy mind were telling her.

"All right, Dani, you stay here. The fire department has to be here soon. It's gonna be okay." Chester pressed a kiss to her heated cheek and then he and James were rushing off.

"Boys, don't!" she heard Mama cry, but then they were inside of the blaze.

"Help them," Dani wheezed, struggling to her feet. Her father was suddenly beside her, trying to support her, but she pulled from his grasp and yanked the hose. "We have to help them!"

She tottered forward a few steps, able to feel the intense heat from the barn. It had gone from being on fire in several places to being almost completely consumed by the blaze. It was too much. It had to *stop*. The normally dark and velvet night was hauntingly illuminated in the unforgiving crimson of the ravenous blaze.

Pointing the hose, she sprayed down the doors, soaking them as well as she could. Even as she blasted them, steam began to rise, drying them out all over again. But she didn't stop. She sprayed straight down the corridor next, thankful that the previous year their parents had taken the time to upgrade the entire hookup and hose so they could clean their trucks more easily. A normal hose most likely wouldn't have had nearly enough output.

A moment later there were a series of bleats and a couple of goats burst out, their little hooves pattering across the ground. Dani gave them a spray as soon as she could see them, tilting it up so the force of the water wouldn't hurt them. The goats reacted to the water just how she hoped, seeing it as a relief and bolting toward it as quickly as they could.

She moved out of their way and kept right on spraying. She couldn't stop. She was going to keep holding onto the hose until they ripped it from her hands.

More goats exited. And more. And then more, until her hazy mind was fairly certain that all of them were safe.

Just as the last ones blitzed past her, new lights flashed behind her. A moment later, the sound of sirens split through the air, and she realized that help had finally arrived.

Relief flooded her, or at least as much relief as one could feel while watching one of the more important parts of their ranch be eaten alive by a seemingly unstoppable force. She kept her hose pointed, wanting to give her brothers some relief from the heat that she knew was in there as soon as she could.

It seemed to take eons before she saw their vague figures barreling forward, animals in each of their arms. She couldn't be sure, but one was big enough to be an older goat while the other was far too small. A cat maybe? She turned her hose on their blackened forms and let out a shout of triumph.

They had done it!

Sure, there was going to be plenty of fallout, and she was sure the dawn would be a grim one, but at least everyone had gotten out—

There was a cracking sound like lightning had struck, but there was no lightning. Dani whipped her head around, trying to find the source of the thunderous sound, and then suddenly fire exploded in front of her.

She was grabbed and hauled backward, the hose flying out of her hands. She heard multiple people around her, yelling loud enough over the renewed frenzy. But they held her still, someone slipping a mask over the lower part of her face. Suddenly cool, dry air was forced up into her nose, and her head cleared a little. Just enough to catch up with the wild panic that had enveloped her brain.

This was like a *nightmare*. Their ranch was *on fire*!

She looked to the barn, to where she had just been standing and was now surrounded by the fire department. They were hooking up their own massive hoses to their water truck, obviously no fire hydrants anywhere out in ranch country.

Where were her brothers?

She tried to stand again, but those same hands pushed her down. They asked her questions, shined a light in her eyes. *Ow*. That hurt.

Where are my brothers?

Finally, she managed to shove the hands off enough to look back at the entrance of the barn. The area that she had been wetting down so dutifully. There wasn't a doorway anymore, just two fallen rafters and a massive blaze that reached above the roof of the building.

"Chester!" she cried, stumbling forward. She had to save them! "James!"

Another step, her head spinning and her legs refusing to move. But she had to keep going. She couldn't stop; she couldn't.

She stumbled to the side and then those hands were back on her again with others. They pulled her up into some sort of vehicle. An ambulance perhaps? She tried to get out, tried to tell them that she wasn't the one they needed to worry about, but then something pricked her arm and the world quickly grew a lot less alarming.

The next thing she knew, it winked out entirely.

2

Benji

*B*enji kicked his boots against the jamb below the door, getting the worst of the muck off before wiping them on the mat outside of the main house. From there he stepped in and toed off those same shoes, setting them to the side on a rack before putting on his house shoes.

The ritual was soothing in its own way, implying that a full belly and relaxation was on the way.

"Oh, hey there darling, do you mind going and grabbing your father from the woodpile out back? I know he likes to taste the soup before I'm done with it."

"He is aware that he has five sons to chop the wood for him, right?"

"Well, four sons really, but you know how he is."

Benji winced at the subtle reference to the youngest Miller boy, who was off who-knows-where, doing who-knows-what. His parents seemed to think that Bryant would be like the prodigal son, but Benji doubted it.

"I do indeed. I'll go get him."

Benji headed out, apparently the only son in the house at the moment. That made sense, in a way. Ben was probably in his newly renovated cabin with Chastity. They'd really made that place into a home, with plenty of room to grow, and Benji wouldn't be surprised if there was an announcement for a new little Miller soon.

The thought of that made his stomach twist a bit. It was strange to think that the next generation of Millers could be starting up soon. It was really a toss-up between Ben and Bart, considering how both of them seemed absolutely head over heels with their gals.

Not that Benji could blame them. Ben had loved Chastity since they were all kids, and Bart's girl was basically a blond bombshell pinup made flesh, and funny as could be to boot. All four of them seemed so happy and to be perfect matches for each other.

It would be nice to have something like that, some special lady who looked at him with love in her eyes. Someone to turn to for comfort and company. A friend, but more.

But in order for that to happen, he'd probably have to leave the ranch and actually interact with people, and that wasn't likely to happen anytime soon.

"Hey Pa, Ma wants you to come taste her soup."

The eldest Miller stood, pausing the swing of his ax. "What kind of soup?"

Benji shrugged. "I wasn't really payin' attention. It smelled like oxtail maybe."

"Oxtail?" he repeated happily before burying his ax into the chopping block and rushing in. It made Benji smile a bit, seeing how his parents were still in love and excited about each other. Made him wonder if he would ever feel that way about anybody.

Even growing up, while he'd found plenty of girls pretty, the attraction had never really gone beyond that. He'd never been pulled to anyone like Ben was pulled to Chastity or caught up in some whirlwind romance like Bart. People were people, and he liked them well enough, but that was mostly that.

And it certainly wasn't for lack of trying. During high school and even for a couple years after, there had been plenty of people who were interested. Whether it was for him or for his inheritance, Benji didn't really know, but none of them had ever gone anywhere because there didn't seem to be anywhere to go.

Heading back in, Benji was all set to see exactly what kind of soup Ma was making when she caught him in the doorway.

"Benjie-boy, I have a favor to ask of you."

"A favor?" he repeated. Ma didn't ask for favors. She either had errands or chores but never *favors*. "What's up?"

"Well, you know that arsonist that's been running about, making a mess of things over the past year?"

"Oh? Did they confirm the fires were all set by the same person?"

Unfortunately, their little town and the town half an hour to the west had fallen prey to several large fires over the previous twelve months. Always a few months apart and favoring different starters and locations, Benji had just figured it was one psychopath and some emboldened copy-cats. Thankfully, all they seemed to be after was property damage, because almost all of the spots hit were on the very fringes of town and no one was hurt.

"Yes, they're pretty certain of it now."

"A serial arsonist, huh. That seems a bit much for out here."

"I thought the same thing. That seems much more like a city issue, but last night..." she trailed off, her face clouding over and Benji noticed it immediately.

The conversation wasn't just small talk, it seemed. There was something serious going on.

"You know the Touhey Ranch, of course."

"Yeah, of course," Benji echoed, his mind spinning off into dozens of possibilities of what was going on.

The Touheys were a family that moved to the area a couple of generations ago and who worked with the Millers on expanding their ranching into new animals and areas of opportunity. But then there was a big falling out and each family went their separate way, but the Touheys without decades and decades of wealth to get them on their feet. They'd struggled and borrowed, and after years of spite, they seemed to be doing rather well for themselves.

Benji didn't have anything against them *personally*, but it was no secret that there was that tension between them. Their ranches were really far too close to each other, and they often ended up competing for the same distributors in the few areas they shared product. Thankfully, the Touhey Ranch specialized in goats and goat byproducts, of all things, so there wasn't too much encroachment.

"Well, they were hit last night."

Benji stared at her, blinked, then stared some more. "They were *hit*?"

"Yes, two of their barns were lost and apparently both of their sons were hurt in it trying to save the animals from burning to death."

Benji shook his head. They were all taught that, in the event of an uncontrolled blaze, that their life was more important than any animals. But if he was faced with the same situation, he didn't know if he'd be able to let horses die right in front of him. Not like that.

"That's awful. You want me to run them food, or something?"

"No, actually," his mother shifted from foot to foot which made his apprehension flare again. Why was she acting so... *fishy*? "I was hoping that, since two of their three children are out for a bit and even their daughter is injured, that you might be willing to dedicate your time to them as long as they might need."

"Ah."

It made sense to ask him. His oldest brother Ben was the lead in the day-to-day function of the ranch and had already taken a vacation at the beginning of the year. Bart was still in the middle of his treatment, and while Benji was sure he'd be happy to help from time to time on the Touhey Ranch, he didn't think his older brother was stable enough or safe enough to help them on his own.

Then there was Bradley, but he was definitely needed for accounting, considering tax season was approaching and they were doing... something that had to do with a... portfolio? Benji wasn't entirely certain, but it seemed very involved.

And lastly, Bryant was gone again, spending way too much money on things that a good Christian boy shouldn't spend time on and doing his best to make it seem like Ma hadn't raised him right.

So that left Benji. The middle of the bunch. The least needed. He felt a bit guilty—thinking that no one in his family ever made him feel lesser on purpose—but it was what it was. Out of all of his brothers, he was just... the middle. Not a leader like Ben. Not sick or strong like Bart. Not smart like Bradley. Not a selfish jerk like Bryant. He was just...

Benjamin.

"Yeah, of course I will, Ma. I wouldn't leave them to just struggle."

He didn't really want to, because the thought of helping a rival ranch seemed like an exercise in shooting themselves in the foot, but he supposed it was the Christian thing to do. And if he couldn't be the smartest, best or brightest, he would at least be the kindest.

"Oh, thank you, dear. Do you mind swinging by tomorrow? I'll call up Elizabeth and let her know that you're on indefinite loan to her. I'll also have Ben ask the workers who would be willing to volunteer to work days over there once you're ready for the bigger projects."

Benji nodded, reaching out to pull his mother in a hug. "No problem. You know you can always count on me, Ma."

"Yes," she said with a contented sigh, burying her face in his dirty work shirt.

Perhaps some people would judge him for being a grown bachelor and being so close with his Ma, but those people could all go kick rocks. He loved his Ma more than anything.

"I do know that," she said giving him an extra pat on the back.

BENJI PULLED his truck up to a modest-looking house with an impressive set of flower beds growing all around it and the path leading up to the wraparound porch. It was much, much smaller than his parents' home, which had once housed five sons and two cousins all at the same time. But it seemed comfortable enough.

He looked around as he got out of his truck and headed up the path. It was easy to see where most of the damage was, with the crumbled remains of two burned-out buildings only a few yards away.

Benji shivered at that. The thought that some sick individual had caused so much damage and hurt made his stomach churn in a way that he didn't like. He hoped they caught whoever the guy was, because it was very clear that they were escalating, and Benji hated to think of more people getting hurt.

Finally, he was at the front door, painted a pale blue to go with the cobalt of the rest of the house, and knocked.

There was a pause and then it was opening, revealing a plump older lady that didn't look all too different from Ma. She had long, silvery hair done up in a loose bun, little fly-aways framing her tired face, and wrinkles carved into the corners of her eyes and mouth.

"Benjamin Miller?" she asked, her voice higher than Ma's with a lighter accent. Their family was newer to the area, so even after a couple of generations, the colloquialisms weren't as ingrained into them.

"That's me," Benji said with a nod. "On loan as long as you need."

She let out the saddest little sigh of relief, and Benji was surprised by how much the sound made his heart ache. That was the noise of someone who had so little hope left that the smallest thing seemed like a big deal.

Footsteps sounded behind her and then a tall, lanky man approached down the main hall. If Mrs. Touhey looked tired and sad, the man behind her looked like almost all the life had been drained out of him. Dark circles hung under his eyes, and his lids were both puffy and raw. He looked like he hadn't slept since the day before and definitely hadn't been drinking enough water.

"Mr. Touhey?" Benji asked, offering his hand.

The man took it in a solemn and brief sort of shake before he spoke. His voice was gravely and strained, like someone who had been holding so much emotion inside of themselves that it had physically hurt them.

"Nice to see you, young man. We're mighty pleased to have you here to help us."

"Yeah, of course," Benji said with a nod. "And speaking of helping you, I figured I'd get right to it. What would you have me do first?"

They looked to each other, as if the idea of him showing up had been so doubtful that they hadn't planned that far ahead.

"Well," Mrs. Touhey said. "A lot of our animals ran off in the blaze. The ones that stuck around are crammed into our minor barn and extra pens, but most are still missing. We think they're still around, so if you'd be willing to search the entire area to round up any you can, we'd be mighty appreciative."

"Yeah, sure. What should I be looking for? Horses? Chickens?"

"Goats and horses mostly. Some fowl but we're most worried about the goats. They're prime targets for coyotes."

"Right. I'll drive around where I can in the truck now. Tomorrow I'll bring a horse. You got a map of your trails?"

"Yeah, yeah we do," Mr. Touhey said, seeming to perk up ever so slightly. "I'll go grab it for you."

"Sounds great. In the meantime, I have plenty of rope in my truck, but I'd like to grab some hay and a water trough if you still have some. That way any critters I pick up can have a more comfortable ride on the way back."

"Oh yes, thank you. I didn't even think of that," Mrs. Touhey said, pointing to the other side of the house. "They're over by the sheds. We salvaged everything we could. Do you need anything else? Water or food for yourself?"

"No, thank you. I ate before I came, and Ma made sure I had plenty of water bottles, including frozen ones for later."

"Ah, she really is a kind woman, isn't she? We couldn't believe she called us, all things considered."

"She's something else, my Ma," Benji agreed with a smile.

He liked to think of himself as a nice person, but he didn't think he'd have the idea to help them on his own. No, that was entirely Ma's doing.

"Well, we're eternally grateful for you helping. It really does mean a lot."

"Don't worry about it," Benji answered with a smile, glad that he had chosen to do the Christian thing. "I'll do whatever I can."

"Thank you. Do you need me to come with you while you get ready?"

Benji shook his head. "No, I'll be fine. You get rest for now. I'm sure that the two of you have been through quite a lot. Take a couple of days, and if I need something, I know where to find you."

"All right, dear. And thank you, again."

Benji just gave her a little tilt of his head and went around the back of the house. He was feeling a lot better about his decision and felt more than ready to kick some butt and help these people out.

Besides, the faster he got things done, the sooner he could get home so things could get back to normal. Not that normal was terribly exciting, but hey, it was his life, and that was all that he could ask for.

BENJI SMILED to himself as he drove one of the many trails back to the main house. He'd been out for around five hours and had managed to find three goats, a rooster, and two chickens. That had pretty much filled up his extended cab, even with the critters tied up for their safety, so he was heading back to the spare barn by the main house.

It hadn't been that hard, thankfully, with most of the animals milling about in pastures, looking like they were expecting something. Benji guessed that was due to the consistent care that the Touhey brand was known for when it came to their goats. While they were no Miller Ranch, they did pretty well for themselves and their animals.

He rounded the corner of some windbreaker trees that had been planted and saw a figure just a bit away, digging out post holes for a new pen. Which they would certainly need considering all the animals he was going to round up over the next couple of days, but it certainly wasn't a job for a single person to be doing.

Benji wondered if they needed help, so he pulled up beside the field and approached the person. As he approached, the figure stood, and he realized that the person was a woman. If he hazarded a guess, he'd be willing to bet that it was the Touhey daughter. She was plump, like her mother, and dressed in oversized overalls as well as a flannel shirt with the sleeves rolled up. Her copper hair was up in a high ponytail on her head, and even from a distance he could see that she had dozens and dozens of freckles. Must have taken after her Pa in that way.

There were bandages on her hand, however, and more just below her elbow. Benji remembered vaguely that Ma had said their youngest had been hurt too, so he imagined that no doctor would want her out in the midday heat doing a job that was meant for a whole team. The least he could do was introduce himself and lend a hand. After all, that was how one was a good neighbor, right?

3

Danielle

*D*igging was just the sort of mindless, menial task that Dani needed. Push the shovel into the ground, step on the edge to make it go deeper. Tilt up. Fill with dirt. Move to dirt pile. Repeat. She could time her breathing to it, slipping into a state where there wasn't much thought involved.

Because when she thought, all she could see were her brothers.

Her hand stung as sweat soaked into the bandages covering her burns. She needed to clean them, but she could do that later. When her head was on right. When it felt like she wasn't about to spin off into a chasm of guilt and despair.

Why them? The arsonist had never targeted anywhere with people before. What had made them choose her family? They never did anything to hurt anyone. They weren't really involved in the town drama. Was it just random chance? Bad luck?

It didn't feel that way.

Dani shook her head, loosening her grip on her mindless state as thoughts crept in. Sighing to herself, she went to grab her canteen only to see someone striding across the field toward her.

She had no idea who it could possibly be and tensed. They'd had plenty of well-wishers and people who had offered to help, mostly by giving her family precooked casseroles and maybe offering a little house cleaning. But the house didn't need to be cleaned. No, the kind of help her family needed was expensive, labor-intensive, and what few people were willing or able to give.

Dani shaded her eyes with her hand and recognition slid into place. She knew that face, although in a more notorious way than anything else, because dollars to donuts, she was looking at a Miller boy.

Which one, she wasn't sure, because once you saw one muscle-bound, stunningly classic Miller boy, then you'd seen them all. They were like someone had hit print five times on that family and just shot out one quintessential, handsome cowboy right after the other. They were the darlings of the town, even from middle school.

Dani wouldn't have minded them being so beloved if it, in turn, didn't make people seem to feel like the Touheys were in the wrong for daring to run their own business. It wasn't like her family was stealing from them or anything, but many in the town seemed to act that way.

The Miller boy continued striding up to her, and she couldn't help but roll her eyes at whatever it was he wanted. He didn't seem to catch it, however, because suddenly he was within socializing distance of her and offering his hand.

"Howdy there," he said.

His voice was nice, as was his strong, chiseled jaw, and his wide cheekbones, and blue eyes. There was a thin but long scar on his chin that wrapped under onto his neck, but instead of distracting from his whole look, it just added to it.

And dang it, was that annoying.

"I'm Benjamin Miller. I assume you're the Touhey girl!"

She looked him over. Part of her knew that she should be polite and see why he was around, but her mind couldn't quite get there. His pleasant, open face just reminded her of how people treated her family like they were encroaching on Miller land when they were just trying their best to provide for themselves. It wasn't like the Millers had a monopoly on ranching.

"You figured that out yourself, huh?" she said caustically.

The man looked surprised at her tone, which she was sure he was. Because everyone was always tripping over themselves to ingratiate to the Millers while no one had ever cared about how Dani thought or felt.

She felt her anger bubble as she recalled some of the things her classmates had teased her for. Gossiped about her. The man in front of her had probably either heard the rumors or added to them himself. No one had ever stood up for Dani back then, and that left her with little to no love for the man in front of her.

"Uh, yeah." There was silence for a moment. "This is usually when you tell me your name."

"Is it?" she asked, leaning against her shovel.

Goodness, what was he thinking in that ridiculously handsome head of his? He was basically a rich, gorgeous man who had the world handed to him, and she was a fat, dirty competitor who was digging a fence post because everything her family had been working towards had gone up in flames.

"If we're going by what my Ma taught me, then yeah."

"I see." She took a long, *long* drink from her water bottle, never removing her eyes from him. "And you always do what your Ma says?"

He seemed utterly confused by her terse responses and honestly, she loved it. It felt like she was taking power back when she'd had so little of it lately. Or ever. There wasn't exactly a lot of adventure or choices when she'd been focused most of her life on helping her family succeed.

"Well, historically, she does have some pretty solid advice."

"I'm sure she does."

He stood there awkwardly, seeming like he was trying to find the right words, before he sighed and gave her an uncertain look.

"I feel like you're having a joke at my expense, ma'am."

"Ma'am?" she countered. "We went to school together. You really don't need to use honorifics with me."

"We did?"

She nodded. "Well, I'm pretty certain we did. The eldest Miller boy was too far ahead of me, but the rest of you were all either right before or behind me." She squinted. "And I never could tell you guys apart. So, which one are you?"

"My brothers and I look nothing alike."

"Sure, you don't."

That seemed to irritate him, and he smirked a bit. She supposed she should maybe feel bad but had any of them ever stepped in and stopped people from teasing her? From making fun of the old used jeans she wore or her waistline? No. And if they weren't actively stopping the bullying from their little gaggle of worshippers, then they were just adding to the issue. That's the way it worked with bullying. There were no gray areas.

"Look, I'm just here to help your family—"

"And no one's stopping you, are they?" She glanced over his shoulder to see the animals peeking over the hay in the back of his truck. Wow, she had to admit, he *was* pretty productive for just one day.

She felt a flash of guilt. She really shouldn't antagonize someone who had obviously just spent the day helping her family, but it felt like her manners were taking a backseat to everything else. Anger, resentment, sorrow, shock, all of that was sitting in the front seat, driving her body while the rest of her mind tried to process everything that had happened that night.

But every time she tried to think about it, she just saw flames. Burning higher and higher, without mercy or restraint. Consuming everything that was important to her.

Shaking her head, she realized that the man had been talking to her again.

"Look," she said, suddenly very tired of him, and the interaction, and the whole situation in general. She wished that she could just go to sleep and wake up when her brothers were happy and healthy, and she wasn't surrounded by reminders of the trauma they'd barely survived. "I need to finish this pen. You should go drop off those animals before going back to that McMansion of yours and patting yourself on the back for helping out the poor folk down the way."

"Did I ever do something to you, ma'am?"

The earnestness of his question surprised her, and she stopped short as she looked him over. It would probably be so easy to give him the benefit of the doubt. After all, he was pretty, and pretty people were always assumed to be good, weren't they?

"I don't know," she replied before turning to dig more. "Did you?"

He let out a very dry snort, and she felt a bit of triumph at getting him to lose his perfect aw-shucks demeanor.

"You're something else, you know that?" he said.

She stood up and affixed him with the flattest glare she could. "The same thing could be said about you."

He seemed surprised at that, staring at her for several moments and seeming to try to think of what to say. But instead, he turned on his heel and walked back toward his truck. Dani dismissed him from her mind as he went, letting him walk out of her thoughts as they settled back into their rhythm.

Shovel in the ground.

Step on the edge.

Fill with dirt.

Put in the pile.

Do it again.

Don't *think*.

Thinking always ended up hurting her, making the tears prick at the corner of her eyes.

Just dig.

4

———

Benji

$\mathcal{B}$enji did his best not to have his hackles raised as he stomped into the main house, his hunger that much more exaggerated by his anger. Of all the things in the world he had expected while helping out the Touheys, a daughter with the bite of a viper certainly wasn't one of them.

He hadn't even done anything wrong! He'd marched right up to her with the intent to help and she'd done everything from dismiss to insult him. He knew that sometimes people were raised differently, but he couldn't think of any sort of upbringing where that was the way to talk to someone who was helping out of the goodness of their heart.

...or because their Ma had asked them to.

But that was beside the point.

"Oh, there you are, dear. I wasn't sure if you'd be stopping by."

Ma came out of the kitchen, a fresh cup of iced tea in her hand. Before Benji could say a word, she turned on her heel and disappeared.

The pause gave him a few more minutes to shove his feelings down before she was back with another glass that she pushed into his hand.

"How was it, dear? Were they hurting terribly?"

Benji took a long sip of his tea, thinking very carefully about how he was going to say what.

"It's not too bad, considering they got insurance and all. I was mostly rounding up some of the animals who got spooked. I'm sure they're still going to lose a few to wild animals or just being lost permanently, but it's not as bad as it could be."

"Oh really?" She took his hand and lead him to her favorite couch; the one that faced the bay window that overlooked a beautiful slice of their land. "That's a relief to hear. Two boys in the hospital, and their girl just barely out of there herself... I can't imagine. I was enough of a mess when you lot all decided to get sick with mono."

Benji chuckled lightly at that. "Yeah, because we had a committee meeting about that and it was a unanimous vote that we all come down with one of the most uncomfortable sicknesses of our lives at once."

She ribbed him gently with her elbow before picking up her knitting. "Don't be cute now."

"I can't help it," he retorted, pulling her into a side-hug. How did Ma always know how to make him feel better? "I am adorable, aren't I."

She made a *harrumph* and busied herself with her work. There was something inherently soothing about watching Ma make something soft and comforting out of thin threads of yarn, so Benji watched her for several moments.

Unfortunately, those same feelings that he had after talking to the Touhey girl began to bubble up, and as much as he didn't want to ruin the mood, Benji knew he needed to speak.

"I don't think that I can help that family anymore."

Ma sat bolt upright and looked at him in surprise. "What? Why?"

Benji wasn't sure what to say. He could tell the truth and explain that the youngest was so incredibly rude and unwelcoming that he felt uncomfortable going back. That he didn't want to do anything to make that vicious woman's life easier.

But that didn't seem right.

Perhaps it was because, deep down, he knew that he should keep helping no matter how nasty she was. That the whole family didn't deserve to be punished for one bad apple. But her words were still stinging at his pride so intensely.

Nobody talked to him like that.

"I just don't think I really will be much use beyond today. And there's some obvious tension with me being a Miller—"

"Really?" she interrupted skeptically. "They seemed so grateful when I talked to them."

Benji swallowed, trying to think of something that would convince her. He knew that dancing around the topic wasn't really fooling her, so perhaps a little more truth would be better than not.

"I just worry that certain characters on the farm would make me act in a sort of... unchristian manner."

"Is that so?" she questioned, her voice soft and gentle.

That in and of itself made him suspicious. He expected a lecture, maybe, or disappointment. Not... whatever she was doing now.

"Yeah. I think it would be better."

"While I am so pleased that you're worried about representing Christ in all that you do, I hope you remember that no one can make you act in any way. You are responsible for your own actions, as convenient as it is to sometimes blame others."

Oh boy. He knew when he was about to be taught a lesson, and he could sense it like his brother could sense a storm.

"If you don't want to help the Touhey family, then that's fine. If you believe that doing so would be detrimental to you, or them, then that's fine too. But what you need to do is take ownership of the choice."

Her wise eyes slipped up to him, and he found himself faced with a gaze that saw far too much. He guessed that's why she was a mother. She seemed to know things that only a Ma could know.

"So, do you take ownership of that choice, Benjamin?"

He paused to breathe in deeply, then breathe out. She was right. He just wanted to get out of going there because the girl was so unpleasant and hurt his pride.

After all, he'd always prided himself on being fairly agreeable. Even-keeled, as some people would say. Maybe it was a part of the middle-child curse, maybe it was just because he liked being likable, but it seemed like a personal affront to be so outright rejected before he even had a chance to speak.

"I... I think I'll give it another try. I guess everyone's awkward in a new situation at first."

Ma smiled ever so gently. "That's my boy. Do you want to eat here, or should I pack you something up to take home?"

"You saved me dinner?" Benji asked with a grin.

"I thought you might be hungry after a long day's work and not want to make yourself something. And if you didn't stop by, I'd have leftovers for one of your cousins tomorrow."

"You always think of everything, don't you Ma?"

"Well, I do have quite a few years of experience under my belt."

"Aw, come on now," he said with a wink. "Not *that* many years."

"Charmer," she accused before getting up and going to the kitchen.

Benji let himself relax as she busied herself with grabbing what she had prepared and then putting it into one of her reusable bags. With a kiss and a hug, he was off on his way.

He didn't stop until he was in his cabin, tossing his boots to the side once again. Taking one of the lids off a container and putting it into the microwave, he collapsed on his couch while he waited.

Once more, that girl returned to his mind. He'd been so affronted by her attitude that he hadn't thought about much else. Like her shining copper hair and burning green eyes. Or the bandages wrapped around her hands and the deep bruise on one side of her jaw.

She had been hurt.

The thought came to him in a jolt, and he couldn't help but frown at it. Should she have even *been* in that field? Working with her hands? He was sure that the metal of the shovel handle couldn't be good for whatever was under those dressings, and he couldn't help but wonder how she had gotten them.

And what she had said... she talked about him as if she knew him. As if she had had a multitude of interactions with him, but he didn't remember ever seeing her once. And it wasn't like she was one to blend in. Even under her oversized work overalls, he could tell that she had a soft, voluptuous form, the type of body that had helped fuel the entire Renaissance. Teenage him *definitely* would not have missed that, even if most of his peers had been drooling over girls with the popular super-skinny style at the time.

Maybe... he had just caught her on the wrong foot. After all, her farm had been hit by an arsonist and her brothers were in the hospital, and she herself was hurt. Benji could sort of understand how that might put someone into a bit of a bad mood. He could reach into the charity of his heart and give her a pass for her behavior.

But still, as he pulled his food out of the microwave and plopped in front of the TV, he couldn't help but hope that he wouldn't have to see her again.

Not if she was going to act that way...

5

———

Danielle

*D*ani barely hummed along to the song playing from the radio, her mind elsewhere as she made the long trek to the city.

When she had first gotten home, there'd been so much to do, so many things to fix, that she thought she wouldn't be able to spare the time to go back to the hospital housing her brothers for weeks. That idea had torn her up inside, making her feel as if she had abandoned them to the frightful reality of being burned over half of their bodies.

Then again, were they even experiencing reality considering they had been put into medical comas?

Thinking that fact so plainly made her breath hitch, and she had to fight not to close her eyes against the memories that swept over her.

She could still see it, still smell it, clear as day. She had been in the ambulance, trying to find out where her brothers were when they'd injected her with something. She'd woken up seemingly only a few seconds later only to find herself in a hospital bed.

Everything had been suddenly terrifying. The air was too sterile, the lights were too bright, and she was alone. She'd tried to get up, but then multiple nurses were streaming in, telling her that she was all right. That everything was fine.

But everything *wasn't* fine.

The only reason her brothers were even in their terrible situation was because she had stupidly tried to save all the animals on her own. She knew that they were insured, and she had always been taught that saving human lives meant more than saving animal lives. But when she had thought about those innocent animals burning in a fiery, agonizing death, she couldn't just stand there and let them roast.

So instead, she had dragged her brothers into it and look where they had ended up.

Her entire life, they'd all been close. Everyone had told them and their mother that they wouldn't be as friendly once they got older, and all sorts of tales about sibling rivalry, but that had never happened. When she had been bullied relentlessly at school, they often were the ones getting in fights to distribute their own justice on the worst of the bullies. She kept telling her brothers that she didn't need them to use their fists, she was plenty good at using her words and none of her detractors were actually brave enough to physically fight her, so it seemed like the wrong thing to do.

Besides, going around and beating people up wasn't the best way to stop things from being said behind her back. Unfortunately, people were always going to talk about the poor, fat farm girl who liked to wear overalls and flannels that were handed down from her older brothers. Annoying, but a fact of life.

Then it was supposed to be that the three of them would all leave after they graduated from high school, no longer wanting to live a life supporting the struggling ranch and heading on their separate ways.

But they hadn't done that either.

No, it'd been her, her brothers and her parents for as long as she could remember.

And she could lose all of that now.

"Hey guys," she said, trying to hold her tears in.

The boys were lying silently in their hospital beds. The hospital unit they were in had worked it out so that the two brothers could be in the same room together.

The doctors had said that their burns were extensive, and they were going to be kept sedated for quite a while, but no one knew quite what they could hear so it was encouraged not to be too morose or weepy. And that was pretty difficult considering she felt like the entire thing was her own fault.

Dani waited until all the nurses seemed to be done with their hourly checkups and the doctors had finished their rounds before reaching into her bag and pulling out a book about Winnie-the-Pooh. It was what their mother used to read to them when they were younger and they, in turn, read it back to her when she would occasionally take ill.

Dani smiled to herself as she remembered how they used to pretend they were in the Hundred Acre Wood back when they were kids. All of them took turns playing the characters like Tigger, Rabbit and Pooh. They had adventures with heffalumps and woozles and climbing trees.

Those had been wonderful times, some of the brightest points of her childhood, so maybe reading them now would help them as much as they helped her.

She opened up to a story about a honey tree. It'd been a while since she'd read it, so she figured it would be a nice place to begin.

"Hey guys, you wanna hear about Winnie-the-Pooh and the gang? We'll start at the beginning."

For a tiny moment, she hoped that they would respond. But they were quiet, the only response being the beeping of the monitors, so she pressed on.

If they could run into a burning barn to save the animals that she was so worried about, then she could at least do this for them.

SHE READ until her voice was giving out. She'd finished several grand tales by then and realized that she hadn't had a glass of water in a couple of hours. Putting the book away, she wandered out into the hall and found the little cubby where they had a water dispenser and plenty of cups.

In a bit of a haze, Dani grabbed one of them and filled it to the brim with icy, cold water. It wasn't quite as nice as the filtered well water they had at home, but it was way better than whatever was pumping through the water fountains back in high school.

Chugging it down, she filled it one more time before going back to her brothers' shared room. They were in beds on opposite sides, a curtain hanging between them that was rarely drawn. Outside the window, she could see that night was falling. It seemed as good a time as any to wrap things up.

Then again, was there anything good about the situation?

Dani shrugged that thought away and curled up in the chair again. She looked over her brothers' forms, the tubes in their mouths, their chests rising and falling. It wasn't a comforting image, but it was something she could hold onto. As long as their hearts were beating and they were breathing, they were alive.

Unbidden, her mouth opened, and a few notes came out. They were melancholy, more breath than tune, but the more she kept on, the more it felt kind of right.

It was a lullaby, the one that her mother always used to sing to them. It had been a long time since any of them were young enough to need it, but Dani couldn't think of a more appropriate time.

It was a simple song that told of where different farm animals and equipment slept. How they were all tucked in and safe until the morning. And every verse always ended with the same promise.

"I'll always love you."

Because she would. Dani knew that to the very deepest parts of her heart. No matter what happened, she would always love her brothers with the fierceness that only a Touhey could muster.

But she wasn't sure she could love herself.

She finished all the verses she could remember, humming when her mind couldn't recall the words. When she eventually stopped, it was pitch-black outside, and she knew she needed to leave if she didn't want to drive sleepy. She knew she could go get a hotel, but the thought of costing her parents more money was loathe to her.

So, she gathered up her things and blew kisses to her brothers, wishing for all the world that she could press her lips to their cheeks instead and they would shove her off for being all clingy.

But she couldn't do that. Not when their bodies were so fragile.

It was a long, long walk to the car. Longer than it should have been, and as she drove home, she felt more alone than ever.

6

Benji

Benji wiped the sweat out of his eyes and from his forehead. He looked over the wooded hill he had ridden to but lost track of the hooves he had been following. It didn't help that the sun had set about ten minutes prior. Where had the day even gone?

He looked to the watch on his wrist. Goodness. He'd managed to chase down two of the horses that he was supposed to catch, but he'd been sure he could find the third after coming across fresh prints in some mud on the outskirts of the Touhey's land. He certainly hadn't meant to stay so late, but he guessed he had just been so focused.

Well, the two horses he caught were still tied to a post next to where he'd parked his truck, close enough so that they could help themselves to the hay and water in his truck's bed. He should probably get them into a barn, and all groomed up. They'd certainly had a rougher time of it than he had.

Turning his own mount around, he let her trot at her own pace across the grassy fields. He'd been so busy being irritated with that cross woman that he hadn't really taken the time to think about how the animals themselves had suffered. The poor things clearly had singed hair in several places, and he was sure he'd find some light burns on them once he looked them over more closely.

It was a shame the Touhey boys had been so hurt, but he couldn't help but be grateful that they had saved a whole lot of beautiful animals from possibly the worst way to go.

He made it back to the two horses in good time, the last of the sunlight disappearing. Pulling his flashlight out, he tied their makeshift lead to the horn of his saddle and slowly walked them back to the secondary barn.

It wasn't anything like his family's mount barn; it could hardly be called a barn at all, but it was the best they had. Benji figured he should talk to his brothers and some of their workers to see if they would be up for a barn raising in the coming week. Goodness knew that the Touheys needed it.

However, despite the small size of the barn, there were two stalls available. Benji led them into their temporary homes, taking the time to fill up the trough with water and get more hay for the feeding bin that their stalls shared.

Once that was all settled, he looked around for any care items. After a bit of hunting, he did manage to find a light switch, and that helped him immensely.

Before too long he had managed to find a brush. It wasn't as nice as the ones his family used, but he had to remind himself that the Touhey Ranch wasn't a multi-dynasty empire like his was. It was easy to forget how someone in the same business could be struggling to just get through the day. Although Benji knew in the abstract that lots of people worried about paying their bills, he'd never struggled with anything like that. And his children would never know that either, and hopefully neither would *their* children.

It was strange to think that their families could have the same livelihood but such different realities, so Benji dismissed the thought. It made him feel… uncomfortable, but he couldn't place his finger on why.

"Hey there, beautiful," he whispered to the first horse as he gently brushed her down and looked for any wounds.

She was a beautiful mix of white, red, and brown. A real dappled girl that his sister-in-law Chastity would have absolutely gone moony-eyed over. The horse shivered slightly but seemed to accept Benji's help. He wished he had a treat to give her, but honestly, after all the trauma she'd been through and the running, she probably just needed to stuff herself on the proper roughage for a couple of days.

He was surprised when he finished up to find no real wounds on her. She had several singed spots and a good chunk of her tail was missing, but that was it. The Touhey brothers must have freed her first, before the barn had collapsed on them. Brave souls.

Once he was sure she was feeling better, he gave the girl a small kiss on the snout. She wuffled gratefully, seemingly very happy to be in shelter, and trotted over to the corner to have some her time. That made Benji feel more accomplished than it should have, but he moved right on to the next horse.

He was a big, silver beast and clearly not as impressed by Benji. His dark eyes regarded the human with a distaste only slightly softened by the fact that he had been fed and watered.

"Hey big guy, I'd like to come in and just look you over, if that's all right?"

Scientifically, Benji knew that the horse couldn't *really* understand him, but there was always a part of him that felt animals knew much more than most scholars would believe. Not that he would argue that with anyone. That seemed like a waste of time if there ever was one.

Carefully, Benji extended his hand with the brush, hoping the big guy would recognize it. He still seemed to hesitate for a moment, but eventually let out a huff and turned his side to the human.

"Atta boy."

Benji went about looking him over and grooming him too. Just like the first, he didn't have any real wounds except for one hard scrape on his upper front leg. It didn't look too serious, but he'd make sure to point it out to the Touheys for when they had insurance bring a vet in. His mane was also terribly singed, and Benji reminded himself to bring grooming scissors the next day so he could snip those bits out. Maybe braid it up and make the guy feel good about himself. He seemed like the type to show off for all the pretty lady horses.

Benji smirked a bit as he remembered his older brothers teasing him for learning all the different mane-styling techniques his mother knew. They said it was silly and that the horses didn't know any different, but their tone changed when Benji helped a cheerleader fix her French braid after she took a bit of a tumble and all sorts of pretty girls came to him for hair-styling advice.

For being a good Christian boy, he certainly hadn't had a shortage of lovely ladies to flirt with. It never really went beyond that because they all wanted commitments that he didn't feel interested in, but it certainly had made him popular. Maybe even more popular than his brothers.

Not that his eldest brother Ben cared one lick. He'd only had eyes for Chastity. Who would have ever thought that would work out someday?

Shaking his head, Benji gave the gray boy a final pat on his flank before setting the brush to the side. He'd clean it the next day when he had time and daylight to find the proper supplies, but for the moment that was good enough.

When he finally made it out of the small barn, it was well past nightfall. He really had lost track of time. He walked up to his own mount, offering her a little bit of the apple he had in his pocket as an apology for keeping her out so long. And also, for their ride home at night. At least she wasn't prone to being spooked like some of the newer additions to their family.

As he was going to swing himself up onto his horse, he heard a soft, lilting sort of sound. One that almost sounded ephemerally impossible as it drifted through the night wind.

Turning, Benji listened hard for the tiny notes. After a moment, he thought he caught what direction the sound was coming from and slowly walked that way, almost wondering if he was hallucinating after a long day's work.

No, the more he followed, the clearer it became. A pretty, dulcet sort of melody with a decided underbelly of melancholy to it. The kind that filled a listener with hope, but also a deep, aching sort of sadness.

After several minutes, he rounded a corner to see the Touhey girl perched up on the fence, dressed in nothing but her nightclothes, which consisted of a very long T-shirt and soft shorts that barely poked out from underneath her top.

He watched as her mouth moved and more of those beautiful, haunting notes came out of it. He realized she was saying words, but he had no idea what language it could be. The syllables were all drawn out as her voice floated up and away into the night air, and it almost felt like some sort of tragic aria.

He stopped dead in his tracks, not making a sound. He had a feeling this was a moment he was not supposed to see. It almost felt like something no mortal should be privy to. And while he didn't believe in magic or witches or anything, it was hard not to see the siren in front of him, bathed in moonlight as she was, and not be enchanted.

She looked so different than the last time he had seen her. Her copper hair was loose down her back in thick curls that caught the gentle wind every so often. That scowl was gone, replaced with an expression so tremulous that Benji wanted to simultaneously reach out to comfort her and also slip away as quietly as possible.

But he didn't do either of those things. He just stood there and watched.

It was like someone had taken the image he had of the girl in his head and turned it upside down. Instead of the rude, bitter harpy he had met, he only saw vulnerability and a soft, feminine sort of beauty that wasn't popular these days, but he had always been drawn to. Her shoulders weren't up by her ears anymore in defense and her features were wide open. Defenseless.

It was only then that Benji spotted the burns along her arms and hands. Some parts were still bandaged, but he could see the top of what was sure to be scars. Had she been in the fire too? He hadn't really heard as much.

But if she was hurt, why had she been out in the middle of the day? The sun was terrible on burns, and he was pretty sure she shouldn't be digging ditches with bandages still on. Maybe... maybe there was more to the acerbic woman than he had initially thought.

Who knew how long he stood there, staring, feeling both confused and enraptured? The Touhey girl sang and sang and sang, the minutes all bleeding into each other, until suddenly she wasn't singing at all, but instead crying into her cupped hands.

Now *that* Benji had definitely not been expecting, and he found himself stuck in another decision. He was clearly eavesdropping on what was meant to be a private moment. If he knew what was good for him, he would turn around right where he stood and head back home.

And yet another part of him couldn't stand to see someone in so much terrible pain. She was so clearly hurting, and each sob from her stabbed through him like a knife.

Before he could figure out either way, she let out a sniffle and then hopped down from the fence. Quickly straightening her clothes, she padded back toward the main family house, leaving Benji to wonder why it felt like his world had just been turned upside down.

7

————

Benji

enji looked over the many bags of chips in front of him, his mind not on his task as he tried to shop for all the bachelor snacks Ma refused to buy for him.

As much as he loved her, it was the one thing his good ol' Ma would never budge on. If he wanted to buy nutrition-less stuff like chips and dip, or popcorn, or other junk, he'd have to do it on his own. She'd always have a home-cooked meal ready for him, but none of that over-processed trash.

And it was trash, but that didn't stop Benji from liking it. He didn't know how he had gotten both the sweet and the salt tooth out of all of his siblings, but sometimes he just craved the worst food.

However, at the moment even all of his favorites couldn't hold his attention. His mind was elsewhere, refusing to focus on the colorful bags in front of him.

It was back at the Touhey ranch, watching a young woman sing into the night like a siren that had been plucked right out of the ocean and placed atop a fence post.

Really, it was impressive that she had been comfortable up there. He hadn't really noticed in those shapeless overalls she wore, but the woman had a pair of thighs on her that were... abundant, to say the least. It would be easy to think plenty of disrespectful thoughts about it, but Benji's Ma had taught him better growing up. People were always people first and should be respected as such no matter how attractive they were or weren't.

Sighing, Benji reached out and shoved an armful of bags into his cart then kept on to the refrigerated aisle where hopefully he would feel more inspired by the dip. He only made it to the corner, however, before a familiar voice caught his attention.

No.

It couldn't be.

What kind of bizarrely impossible chances would allow for the Touhey daughter to be in the same store as him, at the same time, just an aisle over?

Well, he supposed that it helped that there was only one grocery store in the entire town.

Still, he pushed his cart to the side and peeked around the endcap full of tortilla chips. Sure enough, she was standing there with her back mostly to him. She was in another pair of oversized, patchy overalls that spoke of all the hard work she put in on her family's ranch. If he hadn't seen her the previous night in her simple nightclothes, he would have had no idea of the killer, soft figure she had underneath her practical clothes.

"Do you remember if you guys were low on caffeinated or decaf?"

She was talking to someone, the slender girl beside her he guessed. He recognized the brunette from the church. She ran a lot of the extra services, if he recalled right. Keiko... maybe? Her and Chastity seemed to roll together a lot despite their age difference. Strange to see such a soft-spoken, sweet woman paired up with the bristliness of the Touhey girl.

"Just get one of each. Goodness knows parishioners go through coffee like it's holy water."

The Touhey girl let out a harsh bark of a laugh and did as Keiko asked, palming a canister of ground coffee in each hand. Benji was struck again by his uncertainty of what to do. It was weird to creep around the corner of a display, he knew that, but he didn't exactly want to talk to the woman either. What would he even say? Besides, in the light of day, the girl looked more like her harsh, dismissive self rather than the mystical enchantress he had seen the previous night.

Maybe she had a twin? One who was less... *growly*?

The women moved down the aisle, and for a moment he was sure he would be caught, but they stopped in front of even more coffee. They seemed to be silently viewing the selection before Keiko cleared her throat.

"So how are your brothers?"

Even Benji could see how the Touhey girl visibly stiffened and Keiko quickly backpaddled. "You don't have to answer that! I just—"

"No, it's okay. I know everyone is curious." Suddenly the gruffness faded from the young woman's voice while her shoulders slumped. She went from looking ready to hip-check someone to barely hanging on. "They're uh, they're doing as well as can be expected, I suppose.

"They're both in the best hospital in the city. The doctors have been keeping them medically sedated. Apparently—" Her breath hitched and Benji's chest ached at how pained she sounded.

He didn't understand how this wounded, worried woman was hiding within the rude worker he had run into. Sure, he'd met plenty of standoffish people, but she had been beyond that.

"Apparently those kinds of burns are so painful that they can send them into shock and tank their health entirely." She paused to breathe deeply and Keiko reached out to rest her hand on her friend's shoulder.

"You don't have to keep going."

"N-no. It's good. I should talk about it."

"What? The impervious Dani admitting that she might actually need help?"

The Touhey girl—*Dani*—let out the weakest little chuckle that called upon every protective instinct Benji had in his body. "I know. The world must be ending." She paused, her voice tremulous when she spoke again. "Or... at least it feels like mine is."

"Goodness, Dani," Keiko said softly, pulling her shorter friend into a hug. "You've always been so stubborn about never showing anybody else you could possibly be human."

A snort sounded from the tight embrace. "Yeah, because people like to use your weaknesses against you. I thought we both learned that in high school."

"Fair enough." They parted, and Keiko gently wiped Dani's round face of her tears.

Benji could see why Chastity talked so highly of her. The pale woman certainly seemed to have kindness down to her very bones.

"But if you can't trust most people, surely you could talk to your parents. They're going through the same thing you are, after all."

"I know," Dani sighed, pulling away and straightening herself. Just like that, the same impervious girl was standing there, shoulders straight and posture defensive. "But I feel guilty adding anything more to their plate. It's my fault anyway—"

"Hey, slow down there. I know you're not about to try to blame yourself for the fire that a literal arsonist, a *criminal* set."

"Of course not," Dani said with another snort. Now she sounded like the original image Benji had in his head. Good golly, this girl was a rollercoaster of an experience, even from twenty feet away. "But it's my fault my brothers got hurt. I was just so *stupid!*"

Dani's tone was borderline malicious by the end and it seemed Keiko wasn't having it. Immediately, both of her hands were on her friend's thick shoulders.

"Hold on there. That's my friend you're talking about. Now tell me why you think it's your fault?"

"Because it is." Her voice wasn't fragile now, barely clinging onto the edge before devolving into sobs. No, it was full of anger. Of barely checked rage. This woman ran the entire gambit of human emotions like no one else. It reminded him a bit of his brother, Bart, but more vehement. "I went into the barn to save all the animals. I couldn't just let them *burn*, even if we had insurance. I could hear them *screaming*.

"But I wasn't strong enough. I... I couldn't *breathe*. I think I might have fallen over and my brothers dragged me out. That should have been it, but I *begged* them to go back in. To save the goats. Stupid goats! Now my brothers are almost dead because I couldn't remember the most basic rule of fire safety."

By the end of her speech, she was nearly shaking, and Benji suddenly felt so utterly guilty for every negative thought he had ever had about her.

Dear Lord, he had really been a jerk, even if it was inside his own head.

Suddenly her bandages and those burns made sense. As did her abrasive greeting. She was in so much pain, he could feel the deep, raw ache of her regret even from where he was standing. It wasn't right. She had already been through so much.

Keiko seemed just as stirred by the confession because she was hugging Dani again, both of them rocking gently. Well, Keiko rocked, Dani just stood there like a stone, but her shaking did slowly subside.

Benji couldn't really state how long the two of them stood there. People walked around them, giving the two women odd looks, but he busied himself with pretending to check out the endcap. When the two women did finally separate, they started their journey down the aisle again.

He knew that he should go. That he was *definitely* wrong for all the eavesdropping he was doing, but hey... the two girls were in a public place. It wasn't like he was on her personal property, skulking around in the middle of the night.

No, that had been yesterday.

Benji flushed at that and finally got the gumption to walk away. He was almost to his cart when he heard Keiko haltingly take another stab at having a conversation with Dani.

"So, are you guys getting enough help on the ranch? I remember your Ma saying in church that it's still gonna be a bit before the insurance is able to investigate and calculate everything."

"Yeah, they sure are taking their time about it. I just wish that so many people didn't think that 'helping' meant giving us a casserole."

"Oh geez, that bad, huh?"

"I don't know if I would call it *bad*, per se. But definitely a lot of the same. Thankfully some people went above and beyond and got us food that didn't involve being baked in cream. I think I spotted some ribs and some roasted chickens in there."

"That's awesome! It's only been three days, right? So, I'm sure people will be there with more."

"I'm not sure our fridge can handle any *more*. I wish people would be more into physical labor, but beggars can't be choosers. And I know the eighty-year-old church ladies that have the most free time won't exactly be up to moving all the debris that is cluttering up the main part of our barn. Well, what used to be our barn, I guess."

"What? You're kidding me. *No one* has come to lend an actual hand on the ranch?"

Benji waited, holding his breath to see if she was going to lie, but instead, Dani sighed.

"The Millers have actually been pretty helpful."

"What? The Millers? Really? I mean, Ma Miller is the most generous woman I know, but I figured that you guys are kinda competition."

"Only barely. But yeah, she sent one of her sons over to help right away, and they're going to send more workers after the weekend. They're really going above and beyond when they didn't have to."

Huh. So she was grateful. He never would have guessed based on how she had acted earlier. Then what gave?

"Sounds like the Millers to me. So, which son did they send? I think Chastity would have told me if Ben was doing it, and as far as I know, Bart is working on coping with his PTSD. The youngest is still off squandering his money at casinos, so that leaves... either Benjamin or Bradley."

Dani let out a strange sort of huff. "Huh, you really know the Miller boys, don't you?"

"Well, I do listen when Chastity tells me stories. Besides, I went to school with them just like you."

"Well, technically we only went to school with three of them. But yeah. You weren't really tormented like I was though."

"No. The benefit of being mostly invisible. But still, did any of the Millers bully you though?"

Benji stood up straight at that. He never bullied *anyone* in high school. Sure, he and his brothers liked to roughhouse, but they had never bullied anyone. That would be one of the least Christian things to do—not that there weren't plenty of Christians out there who seemed to have forgotten what "love thy neighbor" meant. Besides, Chastity hadn't had the easiest time in middle school, coming up mixed and curvy as she was, so when Ben found out he'd gone on a whole anti-bullying campaign and stuck with it until they both graduated.

"Well, the young one wasn't exactly pleasant. But no, it's not like they directly did anything. But I clearly remember that Benjamin one standing there, not intervening while Jessica fake complimented my outfit."

"Fake complimented?" Thankfully Keiko asked the question so Benji didn't have to.

He vaguely remembered a Jessica... potentially. She was a brunette with hair down to her waist, so she was always coming to him for new styles. They'd gone on a couple of dates, but he hadn't really been interested in anything more. She wasn't really his type.

"You know, when a teenage girl tells you that she just *looooves* your outfit and *wheeere* did you get it? She knew darn well that I was wearing my brothers' old clothes. It didn't make sense to waste money on stuff I would just ruin at the ranch anyway."

"Ah. Maybe he didn't know?"

"How could he *not* know. No laugh like that could ever be nice. And that was just how I met him. We went to school with those brothers for years and did any of them ever talk to us? Did any of them ever do anything but walk around and be popular?

"No. They're just a bunch of rich jokers who've never known what it was like to struggle. They looked down on all of us poor kids while rolling around in their brand-new trucks and designer clothes."

"I'm not sure," Keiko said cautiously. "I seem to recall Bradley being fairly nice. He wasn't the most social, but we were in math club together."

Dani laughed at that. "Of course, you were in math club."

"Hey, don't resent me for actually trying to do extracurriculars."

"I couldn't do extracurriculars and also help my family on the ranch. Sue me."

"I would, but I doubt that'd get me much."

"Hey, was that a poor joke?"

"At least you can recognize a joke. Sometimes I worry that your sense of humor got lost somewhere in the pockets of those overalls you love so much."

"*Ow*. All right, *Jessica*. But still. All I'm saying is those guys rolled with the same people who bullied me. They never stopped anyone who bullied me. They never tried to talk to me or get to know me. As far as I am concerned, they are complicit."

Benji stood there, feeling like his character was being attacked. He didn't remember that instance she was talking about... but that didn't mean it had never happened. And he also didn't ever remember really standing up to anyone. He mostly just ran with his brothers and their close circle of friends.

...but that didn't mean he was complicit, right? It wasn't like he sat there and watched... did he?

"I know high school wasn't easy for any of us, but from what I know of the Millers, they're nice people now. Maybe you should try cracking that door to friendship."

"Please. People have been shunning my family since I was born for daring to exist even near their precious Millers. I doubt someone like him would ever debase himself so much as to be a friend to me."

Well, that just wasn't true! Benji had never looked down on the Touhey farm. Well, okay, maybe he had told a joke or two at their expense through the years. And maybe he had never offered a neighborly hand. Maybe he had been far too amused when a couple of their ventures had fallen through... and hadn't he also pressed Bradley to make a move on one of their clients when their ranch wasn't able to keep up with the output the client needed?

Huh.

Maybe she had a point.

"Besides, I've got you, and I've got my family. I don't need anyone else besides that, because people will always inevitably betray you."

"That's not a very healthy mindset, Dani."

"But it's a true one. People are cruel and selfish, with small shining exceptions every now and then just so they can pretend that they're not as mean as they are. The trick is to accept those moments happily but never hold out the hope for more."

"I, uh... gosh, Dani. That sounds so isolating."

"It's not normally. When my brothers are around."

That seemed to kill the conversation as the two women moved on to the dairy section. Benji quickly retreated, but as he did, he couldn't help but wonder what had happened to that girl. She was so bitter, so wounded, with walls higher than even his brothers.

He didn't know why, but he couldn't help but feel the urge to show her that life wasn't as glum as she made out.

And also, perhaps, that he wasn't as terrible as she assumed.

8

Danielle

*D*ani shut off the faucet, filling up the water canteen for the third time already, and she was still only half done with all the house plants. She wished that she could just unleash the garden hose inside, but that certainly wouldn't work out well for... well... *anything.*

If there was one downside to being a Touhey woman—besides the overabundant figure—it was having a rather virulent green thumb. Ever since Dani could remember, their house had had plenty of plants all around the house. There was the spider queen up on the second floor, hung right beside the wide window at the end of the hall that let in plenty of light. There were approximately a million and one aloes, along with a few other flowering succulents. Ferns, snake plants, cast-iron plants, Chinese evergreens, English ivy along with a plethora of other vined plants. Basically, most of the house was covered in some sort of greenery and even with the large watering can they had, it often took a dozen or so refills to get it all.

Still, Dani had never minded. Her mother took care of them ninety percent of the time, and she or her brothers would pitch in whenever she wanted help. Their father had tried once but had somehow managed to overwater the Queen spider plant and almost killed her. After that, Mom had banished him from ever touching one of her babies again.

But, since both of them were on their way to the city, she had offered to take care of the watering so they could leave an hour or so early. And besides, it would give her something to do that didn't involve digging posts or otherwise exacerbating her burns. She was supposed to put some ointment on them, but she hadn't as of yet.

...she probably should get on that.

Whatever. It could wait until she was done watering. It wasn't like she was like her brothers, all laid up and drugged to the high heavens. If she was, maybe she wouldn't feel so full of guilt. She'd be blissfully unconscious.

A knock sounded on the door, nearly scaring her off the small step ladder she was standing on as she watered some of the hanging plants. They weren't expecting anyone, but she guessed it made sense that a well-wisher might swing by to drop something off. Most of them had come during the first few days, but mayhap they had been busy with work, or even needed to wait until payday.

The door opened by the time she got down to the ground, and she was surprised to see none other than the Miller son step in, looking like he had definitely already gotten started working that morning.

"Oh," he said, eyes going wide as he saw her standing there, one hand on the ladder, the other hand still gripping her watering can. "I'm sorry, I was just hoping to grab some more water. Your mother said I could help myself to your pitcher."

"Right. Of course, she did."

Her entire family was heavy water drinkers, dehydration never really being an issue for any of them. In response, her mother had gotten a truly massive water container that took up half of a shelf of the fridge, and it always had enough for several canteens in it.

Ugh, as much as she didn't like this Miller boy—with his ridiculously good looks and that innocent, 'aw-shucks!' expression that he always wore, and his insane amount of money and his nice clothes—her Ma had drilled it into her to be a good host. So she set her watering can down and extended her hand.

"That's okay. I'll refill it myself," he said.

"No. Have a seat."

Huh. She probably could have worded that a little nicer, but oh well. She was at least somewhat trying.

The man gave her a strange look but did as she asked, handing over his expensive-looking, insulated canteen then going to take a seat at the kitchen table. Dani could feel his eyes on her as she filled the container up and squared her shoulders once she straightened.

She was half-tempted to toss him the canteen and let him be on his way, but a voice in the back of her head whispered that it wasn't enough.

"You said your name was Benjamin, right?"

"Yeah, but most people call me Benji."

"All right then, Benji, you hungry?"

Now he looked even more surprised, and Dani felt a small spike of irritation. What, was it so shocking that she wanted to be polite?

Well, given their last interaction, probably. But Keiko had said to give the man a chance, so she was. Even if she felt like an idiot doing so.

"Oh no, that's perfectly all right."

Dani narrowed her eyes at him, looking him over. While he wasn't as jacked as that one military Miller, he was definitely a sculpted fellow. There was no way that the sculpted fellow wasn't at least a little bit hungry after working all day.

"I literally have enough casseroles and deli meat in here to feed an army. You'd be helping us not waste it, which would be a shame."

"Well... if it wouldn't put you out..."

"I wouldn't offer if it did. You got any allergies I should know about?"

He shook his head cautiously. "Just bee stings, miss."

"Ew. Please, call me Dani. I can't stand any of that miss or ma'am stuff. Reminds me of school."

"Ah, I see."

He didn't say anything after that, just watched as she went about preparing him a plate. It was about as awkward as one would expect, and Dani wondered why in the heck she was even talking to him.

Actually, she was more ignoring him as she scooped from several different glass pans in their fridge then stuck it in the microwave. Although he had his canteen, she still grabbed a tall glass from a cabinet and filled it with a bit of crushed ice from the fridge and lemonade that she had made the night before.

She hadn't been able to sleep, and even going outside to be in the quiet hadn't really helped her, so she'd come in and made a pitcher of sweet tea and one of lemonade before she finally managed to settle into bed. It seemed that while her brothers were stuck in sleep, that bodily function was proving more and more elusive to her.

She set the large glass on the table in front of the still-apprehensive looking man and then the plate a few moments later. With a little more rifling, she soon presented him with a fork, knife, and napkin.

"That's got green bean casserole, taco casserole, some cornbread and I think tetrazzini."

"It looks great," he said before digging in.

As for herself, Dani was all noodled and carbed out for the first time in her entire life, so she settled for pouring herself her own glass of water from the spigot of the water jug. Once that was full, she leaned against the counter and looked over her guest again.

He really hadn't changed much since high school, when he'd pretty much been a heartthrob there. His scar on his chiseled chin was a bit smaller, and his hair was a bit longer than the crew cut he had favored then, but otherwise, he was all around classic American boy.

And entirely out of her league.

Whoa, *whoa.* Why was she thinking about that? There were no leagues at all. She was utterly uninterested in anyone from their town. Or county. Or state even. She was *not* the romantic type.

"So, where are your parents?"

Dani blinked for a moment, having completely forgotten that he was actually sitting in front of her while her mind went on its panicked tangent.

"They're visiting my brothers in the city. They're probably going to stay there for a day or two, so it's just me here."

Why did she tell him that? Probably so he wouldn't make the mistake of coming in and hoping for her mother's soft smile or her dad's terrible jokes. Not that Dad had managed to tell a single joke since the fire.

Dani's stomach squeezed at that, and she turned to the window over the sink while she composed herself. She could *not* get all sniffly and weak in front of the Miller son. Goodness knew he probably already pitied her considering the situation and being pitied burned her skin like acid. She hated it, almost more than anything.

In her opinion, it was better to be hated than pitied. Besides, it was her fault her brothers were even in the hospital, so she didn't deserve anything like pity. No, she deserved punishment. But no one was handing it out. Even her parents, who should despise her for almost killing her two siblings, were understanding and told her not to blame herself.

But who else was there to blame? The arsonist hadn't shoved them in there. Dani had. ...well, not literally. But close enough.

"Hey, are you all right?"

Dani quickly chugged the rest of her water and slammed the cup on the counter. "I'm fine," she said, making sure to turn to him with her composure 100 percent in check. "Why wouldn't I be?"

"Because you've gone through something pretty traumatic and two people that you love very much are currently being treated for something very scary."

Oh.

She hadn't expected an answer remotely like that.

People always hated uncomfortable, emotional situations and would default to empty platitudes whenever they could. But that wasn't what the Miller boy had just said. She looked at him with wide eyes, his words striking down to her core, while he regarded her with a soft sort of patience that didn't make any sense.

Hadn't she pretty much cut off any kindness from him with their introduction? She knew she had been less than pleasant, but he didn't seem to care at all.

"Are you finished?" she asked instead, pointing to his plate.

Internally, she cursed how awkward she was when it came to most socialization. It was like she had spent so long making herself impervious to all the bullying and teasing that she had forgotten everything else. And she really should be nicer to the man who was helping her family so much.

He also looked down at his nearly empty plate and nodded. "Yeah. Thank you, again, for sharing."

"No problem. Like I said, we'd probably end up throwing most of this out anyway."

She didn't mention how her parents rarely ate anything lately. She wished her own stomach would have that kind of reaction, but usually the worse she felt, the more it craved to be filled. But still, even if she was having a complete breakdown, she still wouldn't be able to clean out the fridge before things started going bad.

"Still, it's appreciated."

He drained his lemonade and stood, hooking his canteen to his sturdy looking belt. He was lankier than the older Miller brothers, but still much taller than the other two she had gone to school with. She looked up at him and felt like maybe she was seeing a human for the first time instead of an adversary.

"Feel free to let yourself in for water, by the way. I can't promise I'll be here since there's so much work to do, and I'll probably be the only one on the property for the next few days."

"All right."

And then that was that. He headed towards the door and Dani readied herself to let out a long breath of relief the moment he was gone. But at the last moment, he turned, his eyes intense as they settled on her.

"I know it probably doesn't seem like it, but I promise you not everybody wants to hurt you. There are decent people in this world."

She blinked at him. "Wait, what?"

"I hope you feel safer once your brothers are back. And they will be." He gave her a polite little nod then disappeared back out the door.

Dani stared after him, wondering where the heck *that* had come from. Her mind really couldn't come up with anything, so she picked up the watering can. If she was going to be confused, she could at least be confused and productive.

But geez, the Millers were even stranger than she thought.

9

Danielle

She was surrounded by red. No orange. No, yellow? She couldn't tell. The light was so intense it seemed to burn her vision right where she stood, searing her face in heat that had to be sizzling her skin.

Although she tried to call out, no words would leave her mouth. Only ash, pouring past her lips and down her front. She could feel it, not see it, and the gross chalkiness of it made her cough. She couldn't breathe! She couldn't breathe!

Sinking to her knees, her fingers dug into the ground below her, trying to haul her to safety. But she didn't know where safety was. The only things that existed were the flames and the faint screams that echoed behind them.

There was no escape. She felt the flames close in on her, hungry to claim what had escaped them before. They reached for her, ravenous tendrils that wanted to snatch her up whole. She screamed and screamed, but there wasn't any answer.

. . .

DANI SAT UP WITH A GASP, her head spinning and her stomach protesting *violently*. It was a nightmare. Just a nightmare.

Only a nightmare.

But her hands were shaking as she went to wipe her forehead and she still felt like she was going to vomit. Grabbing her now warm glass of water at her bedside, she quickly chugged it.

Her dry mouth taken care of, she focused on her breathing. She'd learned a few techniques from a school counselor who had wanted to help her through all the bullying she was experiencing for daring to be a fat and poor kid at the same time.

In. Hold it. Out.

Seven counts each.

She couldn't hyperventilate if she forced herself to be mindful and in control of her lungs. All she had to do was count.

Eventually, she was able to calm down her harsh exhales, and she finally looked at the clock. Two in the morning. Geez. Normally she woke up around five thirty, but it felt pretty useless to try to go back to bed. Although fixing her breathing had helped, she still was very much hyped up on the adrenaline from the awful nightmare that had shaken her.

She sat there for several moments, contemplating playing on her phone in her bed, but she knew that would give her too much liberty to think, and at the moment that was the last thing she wanted. In fact, she was pretty sure that she would be happy if she never thought again.

After a brief internal struggle, she decided to get a head start on the chores. Maybe if she finished early enough, she could get some sort of reconstruction task started. Or at least planned out.

Nodding to herself, she slid out of bed and proceeded to put on a pair of comfortable work jeans and a flannel shirt. Normally it would be much too warm for that, but it was still early enough that the cool air would give her a chill once she worked up a sweat.

Having a task on the docket made her feel better, and she grew less nauseous as she filled up her canteen and slung it over her shoulder.

She thought about sitting down and making herself breakfast to start the day on the right foot, but her stomach churned angrily. Maybe that would have to wait until later. Goodness knew a good day's work was usually a sure-fire way to work up her appetite. Moving on, she double-checked that she had her keys and phone both in her pockets, then headed out towards their tiny secondary barn that had suddenly become their primary.

She opened the doors expecting to see a lot of sleepy animals who weren't anticipating her a good four hours early, but instead, she saw a lot of *awake* animals and none other than Benji himself feeding them.

"What are you doing here?" she blurted out before she could think better of it.

Because it was obvious *what* he was doing there, she just didn't know why. It was so early! Had he even left from when she had seen him the previous afternoon?

"I just figured you could use a little extra help since your parents are out in the city. I have a handful of workers coming this afternoon with some of our equipment. See if we can move a lot of the biggest debris off your farm."

She couldn't help it, she stared at him some more. The way he answered her question didn't sound cocky, or "look at me, I'm so good and impressive for doing this for you." No, it was just... matter of fact. As if helping her was just something that was expected of him. As if it was perfectly natural to be up even before the crack of dawn and feeding their livestock beyond what he had already done to help them.

"I, uh... you really don't have to."

"I know. But it's not about having to. I want to."

Why did it sound like he actually did? That didn't make any sense and went against the entire image she had in her head.

Suddenly it was all a bit much for her. Hadn't she had enough to deal with lately? She took another look at him, at his rippling forearms as he held the feedbag, then to the animals before words were erupting from her mouth.

"Okay cool. I'm gonna milk the goats then. You be safe now."

You be safe now? What the heck was that? She didn't know, but she rushed to the back of the barn to grab her stool and a pail and get to work.

A lot of bigger ranches used machines for milking, considering manual took longer and a little bit of skill, but the Touheys had never been into that. Dani agreed with her parents that doing all the milking themselves gave them a much better bond with their goats. Besides, considering they didn't force any of their girls to be pregnant, and made sure that they got proper rest between kids, they really didn't have enough of a herd to justify the upkeep of such a machine.

Thankfully, people seemed more interested in humanely gathered animal products in the last decade, and that was really helping her family. Well, that and their thriving video channel her brother ran of all of their farm animals with their goats being the main stars.

"Hey there, Dipper," she said, going up to one of their calmer girls. Dani wasn't surprised that none of them had really been okay with milking since the fire, but she checked every morning just to be sure. It seemed that the black and white goat was finally ready for it, because she trotted right up to the stool.

Of course, her kid came up as well, figuring he might as well get fed if there was going to be milk going anywhere. It had taken Dani a good couple of years, but her father had made sure to teach her to always make sure that the babies had enough. They didn't formula feed unless there was an illness or other extenuating circumstances.

"Enjoy it while you can," she warned the little guy. He didn't have a name yet, but she knew they'd settle on one eventually. "It's almost time to be weaned."

He just batted his eyes at her, latching on so he could suckle while she worked.

It was relaxing to get back into that routine. There was something calming about the productivity of it all. Maybe it was the knowledge that what she was doing would be pasteurized and then made into a variety of different products.

Of course, her mother wanted to get into raw milk distribution because that was a huge thing as of the last two years. But considering raw milk had a life of about ten days, they didn't quite have the means for that kind of rapid cooling, storage, and then shipping while still remaining profitable.

But that was all right. It was nice to have dreams for the future.

Dreams that didn't involve fires or screaming.

Dani sighed as she finished up with Dipper, bending to press a kiss onto the girl's spine. "Thank you, pretty lady," she said before looking to the next girl.

Normally the goats would be all over their massive pen, jumping around the metal and wooden structures her brothers made, dancing and clip-clopping like someone had hopped them up on caffeine. Mom said that was just how happy goats acted, but Dani was willing to bet they just bred a very *special* line of goats.

"Hey, Cali, you wanna come over?"

California was a beautiful, white-gold goat who was only on her second kid. Both of her births had been singles, about a year apart, but they were still thinking of making her take a rest for a whole year and a half to make sure she wasn't putting her body through too much. Cali had been sickly when she was born, as one of four kids in a single pregnancy, so it made Dani glow to see her thrive—even if her name was a pun by one of her brothers in reference to some song by a band.

Surprisingly, she trotted over too, her relatively new baby bleating as she followed suit. Dani couldn't believe their luck that they hadn't lost a single baby, but when she thought of how that had happened, it made her mood take a nosedive.

"None of that," she reminded herself before delving into her task.

Once more it was easy to sink into the routine of it all, and she found herself blissfully drifting without a single thought. When she finished up with Cali, she called over Delta, who was still reluctant but eventually acquiesced. It was a nice relief, one she had thought was out of her reach for so long. Eventually, she noticed that the familiar sound of milk hitting the metal of her bucket had long since faded.

Looking down, she saw that the bucket was almost completely full. Before she could really register it, an empty pail was placed next to her.

Blinking again—she was doing a lot of that recently—she looked up to see Benji standing next to her.

"Can I take that for you?"

"What?" She wasn't normally this stupid, but geez did the man have a way of confusing her.

"The milk? Your mom showed me your process on my first day here. I can take that for you."

Huh. She hadn't expected a man with such a fancy ranch to know that manually gained milk needed to be cooled almost immediately upon completion. Nodding, she leaned back so he could grab the handle of the bucket and haul it up without splashing. She hadn't thought that through, however, because the movement brought them so *very* close together for a split second.

Instantly she was swamped with his masculine smell. There was the expected undertone of sweat and hard work, but there were also other things. Pine. Teakwood. Something... clean, and subtle. It was all so inherently *man* that she almost swayed off her stool.

"Are you all right?" he asked, standing up and looking down at her like he didn't realize just how stunning he could be.

Stunning? Had she really thought *stunning*? She was definitely up way too early because that was not something that she *ever* cared about.

Before she could answer, however, two of the kids came bouncing up to him, one flipping off the side of his legs and the other straight up nibbling at his jeans.

"Whoa, hey there little ones. You've got some energy for it being so early in the morning." He set the milk down and tried to gently shoo them off, but that resulted in both of them thinking it was playtime and another one bounding over to enjoy the fun.

"The best strategy is just to get out while you can," Dani said, unable to stop herself from cracking a smile as she watched them try to weasel a game out of the stranger.

"Thanks, I'll try that," he said with a short laugh before walking out of the pen with the bucket carefully in hand.

The kids bleated like they were truly slighted, the spoiled little things, but they quickly forgot about the man as Dani called over one of their moms. Soon it was business as usual as she filled up another milk pail.

But then Benji was right there, bending to take that one too. This time she anticipated the move enough to scoot her stool back, but that still brought the side of his head so dang close to hers. His hair was surprisingly pretty and healthy for a busy rancher—even if he was rich. A deep brown with a hint of red to the ends, it caught the light of the barn way better than it ever should have. His red was so different from her own copper, her hair being more orangey like desert earth whereas his was like deep blood.

Oh boy. She was *not* waxing philosophically about hair, was she?

Thankfully, the kids trotted up again to get her mind off of things her mind should not care about at all. And by trotted up, she more meant trotted up with mischievous intent.

"I think they like you," she remarked, resting her chin in her hand as she watched one jump up and try to headbutt him in his middle. "I guess there's no accounting for character in baby goats."

Normally a phrase like that would be a vicious barb from between her lips, but instead, it sounded almost playful. What the heck was wrong with her?

"Hey, most people like my character just fine, thank you very much," Benji answered, the corners of his eyes crinkling as he sent her a crooked smile.

Oh Lord on High, did he think she was *flirting*? She wasn't... right? Dani had never flirted a day in her life, and she certainly wasn't going to start on a Miller boy.

"I'm aware. But I'm not like most people."

"Now that is something I definitely would agree with," he said, his smile increasing before he strode off with the pail in hand.

Dani stared after him, surprised by his admission. What did that mean? What did any of his strange behavior mean?

And why did she care so much?

It was all so weird and confusing and not what she expected, so she tucked it away to return to milking. Problems like handsome, rich and confusing helpers could wait until after six a.m.

Yeah, that seemed like a good rule.

10

Benji

*B*enji straightened, popping his back with a long stretch as he stepped down from one of the machines they had driven over from the ranch. Four of their workers were also helping, finishing up the last of cleaning up the burned remains of the Touhey primary barn.

Two weeks.

It'd been two weeks since he first started helping them and there was still so much left to do.

Thankfully, the insurance adjusters had finally come to take pictures and collect the evidence from the Touheys and the police. That had been four days previous, and he was hoping they wouldn't drag their feet on calculating the payout and distributing the funds.

Due to the great insurance the Touheys had sprung for, they stood to make a tidy sum. It was enough to cover all they lost plus the medical costs for their sons, and maybe invest in a few more animals. If Benji knew a way, he'd personally add to it, but he knew that the

Touheys were a proud family and most likely wouldn't take a monetary handout like that when they had an insurance check in hand.

As for Dani... well, while she was warming up to him, she was still... *prickly.*

Or maybe prickly wasn't the right word. Maybe it was more aloof. She didn't instantly abrade him on sight anymore, and they had actually had some good almost-conversations.

Granted, those kinda-talks were few and far between. Once her parents came back, it seemed that she was always working on some project or another for her Ma and Pa. And it felt like it would be creepy to stalk her across her own ranch, so he just waited for chances to run into her.

Okay, so maybe he occasionally would run her a fresh water canteen in the middle of the day. And maybe he brought her sunscreen once or twice when she accidentally left it in the house. And maybe he also brought her lunch, interesting news, updates on his progress, and general questions if he was curious about something.

He often tried to keep his questions light, unpressured. How she was doing. How the goats were doing. If she needed any help milking, etcetera... etcetera...

Ever since her parents had come back, she hadn't needed his help with the animals. He tried once or twice, but she usually told him that she was fine on her own and he was no doubt needed for more important stuff with the barn rebuilding and repairing the power supply to that half of the ranch.

Benji knew that her family had expected to hire an entire contracting team to take care of all the clearing and rebuilding. He was sure that his and his family's help was saving them thousands of dollars. Which did actually make him feel pretty good. No one on the Touhey ranch treated him like a middle child, like a backup to Ben. To them, he was the Miller son who was in charge of everything getting them through each day.

Perhaps it was a little bit pathetic that his ego was stoked by that, but it was what it was. Besides, he didn't care about that nearly as much as he cared about... doing whatever it was he was trying to do with Dani.

Make her like him? Maybe. He had always been well-liked in high school, and he enjoyed being popular. It grated on his nerves for someone not to like him just because. But maybe he just wanted to make her feel better. It hurt to see her so wounded, so haunted. He didn't know what it was about Dani that made him want to protect her, but whatever caused that feeling was quite strong.

Or maybe he just wanted to fix everything, and have it tied up all neat with a bow. As Ben's second-in-command and the problem-solver of the ranch, he hated to leave things broken or malfunctioning. When there was a mess, he was the one who came in and fixed things. Before Missy was in the picture, he was really the only one who remotely knew how to interact with Bart. Not that Dani was anything like Bart, but he had a feeling she had at least a little bit of PTSD from that fire, and that was half of her issue right there.

Benji felt a bit of remorse that he had apparently been in high school with young Miss Dani without noticing her. It almost seemed impossible. Between the intense look in her eyes and the sort of sway she had to her wide hips even under those shapeless clothes, she was exactly the type of girl to catch his eye. Even when he was young, he knew that—while he was attracted to a broad range of bodies—there was one particular type that could always be described as his favorite.

And Dani was definitely it.

Not that he was helping her just because he found out she had such a *body* under those work overalls. Or the determined set of her pretty face. Or anything having to do with looks.

...all of that didn't hurt though.

Benji shook his head at his own silly thoughts, but the movement had the corner of his eye catch on something colorful in the distance. Turning and narrowing his gaze, he scanned the horizon for whatever it was.

He saw nothing for a second. And then nothing for another second. He sighed and told himself that he was just looking for another way to keep himself on the ranch longer, even though the sun had set a good ten minutes earlier.

But then it happened. The tiniest lick of color and light crackled above the tree line for only a breath and then disappeared down below the wall of foliage. All it took was that glimpse, however, and Benji's heart locked up like someone had shocked it.

Fire!

Everything happened at once then. He let out a cry of alarm to wake up the sleeping Touheys, then yanked his keys from the ignition of his vehicle and scrambled for his cell phone. He had 911 dialed before he even realized that he had unlocked his screen, and breathlessly he told them that the arsonist had struck again.

They asked him questions, so many questions, which Benji answered breathlessly. He wasn't even aware of what he was doing until he reached the powerful hose that the Touheys usually used for cleaning their barns. It wasn't nearly long enough to reach as far as he had seen in the trees, and it wasn't powerful enough to fight a true inferno, but it could help with exactly what Benji had in mind.

He tramped down panic as he raced to the edge of the large vegetable garden where the grassy pens were. Cranking the release on the hose, the intense pressure that had built up in it during his run made a jet of water shoot out in front of him like a blade.

Good.

He didn't stop, soaking the area of the pen until he could see there were expansive puddles starting to fill it up. It would be unusable for a couple days, sure, but it would be unusable for a whole lot longer if the fire got to all that grass without anything to slow it down.

Some back part of his brain heard footsteps behind him and then Dani was beside him, panting hard. He could practically smell her panic and fear from where she stood.

"W-what's happening?"

He simply pointed to the trees, and her breath caught even further.

"No," she said, sounding absolutely wretched.

It was almost enough to get Benji to drop the hose and make sure she was okay, but he knew that wasn't what she needed at the moment. No, she needed security. She needed to be protected from the blaze. And if all he could do was make a wet perimeter while the fire department raced into the woods, then he would dedicate himself entirely to that.

Mr. and Mrs. Touhey came racing up next, their steps considerably slower than their daughter. Mrs. Touhey let out a shocked little warble that told Benji she saw exactly what he did, while Mr. Touhey only gave the tiniest little gasp before starting to sway.

"Whoa, Dad!" Dani cried, gripping her father.

Between her and Mrs. Touhey, they were able to get him upright.

"Not again," the older man whispered, making Benji's heart ache.

In the weeks he'd been with them, he'd learned the Touheys were good, kind people. A little quiet, a little standoffish maybe, but *good*. They didn't deserve this!

"How can this be happening *again*?"

"Maybe it's just a forest fire," Benji said, wanting to comfort them but not wanting to stop spraying the next pen. He was trying to make an entire perimeter in case the fire really got going. He knew it wasn't entirely uncommon for the flames to jump and get picked up and carried dozens of feet or even yards to cause an entirely new blaze.

"There's no such thing as *just* a forest fire." Her hands went around the headpiece of the hose and tugged it gently. "Come on, Mom can do this. We should ride out and help the firefighters."

That seemed to spur Mrs. Touhey, and she jolted to life. "What? No! Did you learn nothing from the first time? Dani, let the professionals take care of this!"

"And what if they don't come in time!" Dani yelled back.

Benji could see so much in her face, shining flushed in the darkness of the night. Her bright eyes were flashing defiantly, wisps of copper hair whipping around her head. She looked like some sort of ancient, Amazon warrior who was about to gear up for battle. Benji would pity anybody who was her enemy, except the fire wasn't an anybody. It was a force of nature. An unstoppable combustion that didn't know mercy or fear or love. It just consumed until there was nothing left.

"What do you even think you could do if they didn't?" Mrs. Touhey argued.

It was the most vivid, the most animated even, that Benji had ever seen the woman, and he realized that he had really only seen the numbed, half-alive aspect of their personalities. How strange.

Suddenly Dani was whirring to him. "Your truck, it has that big water tank on it, right? You hooked it up for your workers?"

"Well, yeah," Benji answered, feeling swept up in her fervor. "And the pressure washer."

"Then we can use that! And the sandbags soaked in water. We can set up a perimeter before it gets to the maples and hackberry trees."

Benji vaguely remembered that Mrs. Touhey mentioned they used those for syrup and berries for their pies and other confections. Nothing that they depended on commercially, but certainly something that they looked forward to.

"Dani..." he warned cautiously.

But then she was stepping forward until her body was close to his, face tilted upward so that he was looking right down in it. He saw so much there. Determination, fear, vengeance. It all twisted up into something beautiful and intimidating and it stole his breath away.

"All right, I'll help, but we stay away from the fire. If we get too close, I throw you in the truck and we come right back."

"*What?*" Mrs. Touhey cried, clearly surprised.

But Dani just let out a whoop and handed her the hose.

"Make sure you make a really good perimeter," Dani said before rushing off.

Although he was loath to let her disappear off into the darkness, he knew he had to run and get his truck. So that was exactly what he did, using his phone as a flashlight so he could cut across the ground without accidentally rolling his ankle or ending up in a ditch.

Benji reached his truck in possibly record time and threw the door open, clambering to drive back to the storage shed that had been shown to him on the first day. He knew that was where they kept a good chunk of their supplies and was willing to bet that Dani had bolted straight there.

Sure enough, he was right. The double doors of the small thing were flung open and Dani was standing inside, panting again as she picked up sandbags and threw them out the door. Those things certainly weren't light, so it was impressive to see her tossing them like it was no big deal. If she could handle the heavy bags so easily, it was easy to picture a child on her shoulder, or perched on her back—

This was *not* the time to be thinking about that.

He didn't think there was a good time to *ever* think about something like that.

There was a *fire*.

Shaking his head, he picked up the bags she had tossed out and threw them into the back of the bed, beside his water tank. Between the two of them, they got a good number of the bags into his truck before he went to fill his tank from the pump next to the well. It had been a little confusing to use at first, but in the weeks he'd been on the Touhey ranch, he had long since learned how.

He was completely winded by the time they were all set, but there was no break. Dani practically vaulted into the truck, moving her body with a strength and assuredness he hadn't seen her move with previously. She slammed her seatbelt on and looked to him expectantly.

"Are you sure you want to do this?" He knew what her answer would be, but he felt that he had to say it. It was kind of like he was caught up with the maelstrom that was Dani, and he suddenly could only watch in awe as she swept across him and the entire situation.

"Yeah. But if you're not, move over. I'll borrow your truck."

She really was something else, wasn't she? "No. I'm in. Just thought I'd be polite."

"Yeah, well less of the politeness and more of the pedal to the medal, if you don't mind."

From anyone else, it might have been rude, and maybe it even *was* rude, but he was too caught up to care. Everyone had always said he was laid back, but he just generally liked watching strong-willed people do their things.

"Aye-aye, ma'am."

They peeled out, cutting across the worn-path and to the tree line. Now the fire was really a sight to see, peeking above the canopy and turning the black night sky into a foreboding indigo. Normally he loved that color, but with the underbelly of crimson and vermillion, it certainly wasn't a welcome shade.

They went as far as they could into the trees, ending up in a grove that Dani quickly said something about being their harvest point. Then she was shooting out of his truck and grabbing some sandbags.

The fire was still plenty far away, but Benji could feel the heat of it ever so faintly on his skin. Birds and other animals either rushed towards them or up into the sky, eager to escape the inferno that was quickly building.

Benji was no fool. He knew what they were doing was dangerous. The fire could jump, or have a flash, or do any number of things that could make their location go from "far enough away" to deadly in a second flat. Which meant they needed to work fast. Benji had already figured out that Dani wasn't going to back down until she felt that she had done enough. And if that meant he had to rush through setting up precautions to try to save this land for her family, then he would do just that.

"I'll hook up the pressure washer," Dani said as soon as they were down to the last few bags.

Benji just nodded, not even taking the time to wipe the sweat from his eyes and finished up the task. It was growing warmer by the second, and the hair on the back of his neck was standing on end. His entire body was trying to tell him that he was in danger, that he needed to run, but he was determined to do whatever it was that he needed to do to make sure that Dani got whatever she needed out of her system and got back to her parents in one piece.

Almost as soon as he stood, the sharp sound of the pressure washer issued behind him. He took a step back and saw Dani planting her feet before unleashing the full force on the line of bags.

They quickly grew dark with water, forming a formidable line curving around the half of the grove facing the blaze about a couple of feet high. It wasn't enough to stop a full forest fire by any means, but maybe it would buy them enough time for the fire department to get there.

Normally Benji loved living so far from town, the peace and quiet helping him relax after long days of trying work. But at the moment, he couldn't help but wish that they were closer.

"Here, let me take over for a minute," he offered, extending his hand to Dani.

"No," she answered, voice so fierce with determination, it actually surprised him a bit. "I have to do this. I'm gonna keep it back."

He watched her, standing there like a warrior staring down her enemy. She looked beautiful, powerful even, but she also looked a little bit like she wasn't really there.

Not physically. She was obviously standing there, feet planted, shoulders back and cherubic face smeared with sand and dirt. But her gaze was elsewhere, like she was seeing something he wasn't, and even her words seemed to be talking to someone else.

His gaze went nervously to the fire to her and back again as she soaked the earth in front of their little fire-line. Now there was a wall of orange glow in front of them, and he could definitely feel the heat rising. While there was a level he was willing to indulge, he wasn't going to let her risk her life. Her parents already had two sons lying in hospital beds. They didn't need their little girl there too.

"Dani," he said again. "The water is out in my tank. We should head back."

As if to echo his sentiment, the faint warble of sirens sounded in the distance, the color of their lights disrupting the night just the same as the fire. It was like the cavalry was coming in and Benji let out a long sigh of relief.

But Dani didn't seem to care. She threw the pressure washer to the ground and grabbed a shovel from the back of his truck, running forward. Benji barely managed to catch her around her waist, but she fought and kicked at him wildly.

"No! Let me go! I have to save them! I *have to save them!*"

"Save who?"

But she was kicking wildly at the air, throwing herself from side to side to try to wrest herself from his grip. "I... I..."

She seemed to be confused, her words fading into halting sobs. He was instantly reminded of his brother when he used to go into one of his fugue states, so he was beginning to think that maybe Dani wasn't in the here and now.

"Hey, listen to me, okay? Let's take you home. The fire department is here. They'll take care of it, I promise."

"No! *No, no, no!*"

Her thrashing was growing weaker as she tired herself out, and Benji found himself hauling her up and over his shoulder like a sack of potatoes. She was quite solidly built, but after years of working on the ranch, she wasn't anything he couldn't handle.

He felt a bit guilty as he dumped her in the passenger seat of his truck, making sure to slam the child safety lock on her side and sliding over his hood to get to his own door. Somehow, he managed to get in and pull the truck away as Dani threw herself against the door, sobbing loudly.

"It's happening again," she said between wet gasps. "It's happening again, and I still can't do anything to stop it."

"Shhh," Benji soothed, reaching out to comfort her. His heart utterly *ached* at the sounds she was making, and he once more felt guilty for every single bad thought he had ever had about the poor girl. She was clearly so strong, so brave, but had life yanked right out from under her. "It's gonna be okay, I promise. Look, the firefighters are right there."

He pointed across her, but instead of looking at the trucks as they rushed by, she grabbed his arm and held it to her body.

If perhaps it were any other moment, Benji would have let himself get distracted by her lush form pressing into his arm. But it certainly wasn't that kind of moment, so he stored those thoughts to think about later, on his own time.

"I can hear them," she whispered.

"Who?"

"My brothers."

"They're not there. I promise. Okay, Dani? They're in the hospital right now, safe and sound."

A keening noise issued from her lips. It was even worse than the sounds she had made earlier. "But... I hear them."

"I know, but they're not there. I swear it."

She nodded dully, sinking into softer whimpers. "I could have saved them..."

Benji didn't know what to say to that, so he just let her hold onto his arm and cry as long as she needed.

And if she needed anything else, he'd do that too.

11

Danielle

*D*ani woke up with a groan, her head feeling full and heavy like someone had filled her entire skull with wax. She always felt like that after taking a sleeping pill, which was why she usually avoided them, but after her third night in a row with only a couple of hours of sleep, she'd given in to a little help.

Her eyes fluttered open, seeing a form above her. While it was unusual for one of her parents to be in her room, waiting for her to wake up, she'd found her mom asleep in the rocking chair in the corner of her room more than a couple of times since her brothers had been injured.

But as her vision cleared, she realized it very much *wasn't* her mother. In fact, the person was probably the farthest she could get from her mom considering that Benji himself was staring down at her in concern.

"What are you doing here?" she cried, sitting up with a jolt.

"Hey, there. You feeling okay?" he asked, handing her a glass of water.

"What I'm feeling is *alarmed*."

"Your parents are cleaning some things up and talking to the police. They asked me to watch you while you slept. We didn't realize you'd taken a sleeping pill before waking up and dealing with all the excitement. Which makes sense given—"

"Given what?" she cut him off sharply, already feeling like far too much had happened far too soon after she'd woken up.

"Well, uh, given your behavior last night."

Last night? What could he be—

Oh.

Memories finally came rushing back to her. There'd been a forest fire last night after she'd taken her sleeping pill and gone to bed. Benji had sounded the alarm and jolted her out of her sleeping-pill induced dreaming.

Dani groaned, trying to recall all the fuzzy details. The night took on a syrupy sort of haze in her mind, replaying like an old VHS that had one too many scratches on it. While there wasn't a clear storyline from start to finish, there was enough to tell her that she hadn't been acting entirely... *lucid.*

"Oh, my dear Lord on High," Dani groaned, sinking her head onto her knees. She was *so* embarrassed. Like cheeks burning, ears red, wanting to sink into the ground and never emerge kind of embarrassed.

He must think that she was absolutely insane. Off her rocker. *Mental.* Who ran *toward* a fire? Especially since her brothers had almost been killed doing the exact same thing.

Well, if she was going to be forced to actually live through the humiliation, then she might as well try to get it over with.

"I, uh, I guess I owe you an apology then."

Benji's eyes went wide, and he looked genuinely surprised. "Huh? An apology for what?"

Either he was really good at being polite or he was an alien, she wasn't quite sure. To be fair, he was ridiculously handsome.

"You know, for being, uh, prickly in general and maybe a little bit insane last night."

He just shrugged, taking the empty glass of water from her hand and sliding a cereal bar into her grip.

"There's really nothing to apologize about. Stress, plus trauma, plus a fire seems like a pretty good reason to cry to me."

Oh goodness, she really had cried, hadn't she? Like a baby. She was sure he was going to judge her for that forever. Silly little Dani Touhey, who burst into tears in the middle of the woods like a lunatic. Goodness knows that she had long since learned that crying in front of a bully was to give them the ultimate satisfaction that they had done their job right.

Huh... did that make the fire a bully?

She didn't know, she was getting her metaphors and reasons and everything all mixed up. Maybe it was the sleeping pills. Or maybe it was because her worst nightmare had come true. The fire had returned.

"Are we being targeted?" she heard herself ask Benji before she could stop herself.

Ugh, she sounded so *weak*. So scared. But that was probably because she was. When the yellow and orange glow of those ravenous flames had lit up the night, somehow, she was right back at the barn.

His face crumpled a bit more and his hand came forward again to grip her free one. She stared at the gesture, trying to figure out why he was comforting her when he should be running for the hills.

But his calloused fingertips winding around her palm gave her comfort. Like they were grounding her and shaking the last bit of last night's fogginess from her mind. She had kept a solid distance from him ever since that morning in the kitchen together, when he'd first said such strange things to her, but she didn't have it in her to pull away.

She didn't want to pull away.

Normally her walls were so high and she was so intent on never letting someone outside of her family get close to her, but it felt pretty nice to have him offering her that small bit of solace when she was so afraid of what his answer might be.

"I don't know. They're investigating. It does seem unlikely that it is a coincidence, but I don't want you to worry."

Dani outright snorted at that. "A serial arsonist is possibly targeting my family. I think worry is a foregone conclusion at this point."

He smiled ever so slightly. "I could see that. But I guess we should try to keep it down to a minimum until we know what's going on." He gave her hand a gentle squeeze. "You want another glass of water?"

She nodded and he stood, grabbing the glass and heading out. She listened to him walk to the bathroom then turn the tap on, so she hurriedly dug in her nightstand for her compact mirror.

It was there for when she woke up with a painful pimple on her face, but she quickly used it to straighten her hair and wipe the gummies from her eyes. Good gracious, she looked rough. Like... well, like she had tried to take on a forest fire by herself while in a partial sleep-aid induced fugue. Granted, she couldn't blame it all on the meds. A good chunk of it was definitely related to it being a fire, she knew that much.

Maybe she should see a therapist?

But she would have to see one out of town which meant even *more* trips into the city. And she just didn't have time for that.

Benji returned with a full glass, handing it to her before sitting back in the rocker that had been pulled close to her bed.

She eyed him suspiciously, her head feeling all muddled up. "Why are you being so nice to me?"

He smiled crookedly, giving her a look that no doubt had melted many a girl's heart throughout his life.

"Am I really being 'so nice'?"

Well, she wasn't going to let him tease her like that. She affixed him with a critical expression.

"You helped me last night. And you brought me here—that couldn't have been easy. You also sat here for goodness knows how long so my parents could deal with things, and now you're waiting on me hand and foot."

He chuckled at that. "I would hardly call getting you a glass of water waiting on you hand and foot."

"Excuse me, *two* glasses of water," she countered.

"Ah, of course. *That* makes all the difference."

"You bet it does."

The exchange startled a little laugh out of her. Was she really... bantering with someone? Let alone someone who had contributed to— or at least hadn't prevented—her getting bullied in high school?

"But seriously. I haven't exactly been the nicest to you. And it's not like we got off on the right foot. I wanted you to know that I wasn't your fan and made sure you knew it."

Another chuckle from him. "Don't worry. Your intent came across quite clear."

"So then why?"

He shrugged, looking a bit uncomfortable, but she couldn't help it. Her natural sense of the order of things told her that something was amiss. This wasn't how things were supposed to go.

"Maybe I thought that you deserved a little kindness."

That was possibly the last thing she expected to hear. "Why on earth would you think that?" she blurted out before she could think better of it.

In response, he sat back, giving her the tiniest of shrugs. "Just what I happen to think."

"That doesn't make any sense though. No one's kind to a stranger without wanting something."

At that, his kind expression crumpled and a melancholy look entered his eyes.

"I have to be honest with you, Dani, that's a real sad way to look at the world."

Now it was her turn to shrug. "It's just what I've observed in my twenty-odd years of life. I know we may have walked different paths, but even you've gotta know how terrible people are."

"What do you mean, even *me*."

She could tell his tone was shifting toward playful, trying to break the tension that had built up between them.

"You know exactly what I mean," Dani countered, feeling herself grin ever so slightly.

"I assure you, I definitely don't. Care to elaborate?"

She gently chucked her empty water glass to him in response, and he caught it, looking much more relaxed now that she wasn't asking him questions. But it wasn't *her* fault that he was turning her understanding of everything on its head. She wasn't sure if it was some sort of weird trick—like the time Dillon had pretended to ask her out freshman year, or the time Suzi had pretended to be her friend and invited her to sit with her crew at the lunch table—or if he was just as out of his mind as she was.

Now that she thought of it, didn't one of the Miller boys have something a bit wrong with his head after he came back from the war? Maybe they all were a little screwy.

Dani frowned at that. That wasn't a nice thing to think, especially considering how prolific PTSD was among veterans and other trauma survivors. Even if no one could hear her thoughts, it would do her better to think more respectfully of the man.

"You okay there?" Benji asked, noticing her frown before she could tuck it away.

She nodded quickly. "Yeah, but I think my bladder is trying to get back at me for being in bed so long. You can clear out if you like. I'll handle myself from here."

The handsome man hesitated, whether it was because he wanted to say more or if he just didn't want to leave, she didn't know.

"You sure?"

"Yeah. I'm fine now. Thanks for helping my family. I mean it."

"T'wasn't nothing. Just being neighborly."

"Oh, is that all? I wasn't aware driving directly into a forest fire was considered proper etiquette."

He actually blushed at that, and if that wasn't the most adorable thing she ever saw, she didn't know what was. *Geez,* this guy was a charmer. If she didn't know better and have a chip on her shoulder the size of Mount Everest, she could see herself getting swoony over the insanely rich bachelor.

Because that definitely wasn't *actually* happening. She was much too smart for that.

"Well, I guess I may have improvised that part, but I'm glad I was there. I overheard the firefighters telling your folks that our fire break did actually help stop the spread of it. You know, along with all of their work."

Dani smiled at that, feeling herself ease. "I'm real happy to hear that."

"Me too."

He continued to head out but stopped by the door and turned around. When he looked at her, his gaze was almost too intense. What was he thinking? She found herself wanting to know.

She didn't have to wait long.

"Actually, considering the most recent events, I'd like to ask you a favor," he said.

Here it was. *Finally.* The reason for all the sweetness and sugar. She leaned back, feeling much more centered now that she knew he wanted something. That computed in her rules of the world.

"What's that?" she asked, trying to ignore the disappointment in her gut.

"You try to be safe out there, okay?"

Wait... *what?*

But before she could ask anything else, he was out the door, and she could hear him going down the stairs.

That brief moment of confidence where she thought she knew

what was going on faded with his footsteps. She thought she had him all figured out, but he wasn't acting anything like he was supposed to. Did that mean something, or did fires just throw everything out of whack?

She didn't know, but she felt her curiosity piquing like it hadn't in a long time. Sliding out of bed, she headed to her bathroom so she could wash up and deal with the repercussions of her actions. And, potentially, ponder a certain snobby rich guy who wasn't acting like a snob.

Not lasciviously, of course. Her cheeks burned at the very thought. It was just that she did a lot of good thinking in the shower. It wasn't like she'd be imagining him—

Dani stopped and shook her head. It was clear that she still wasn't thinking like herself.

It had to be the sleeping pill.

...right?

12

____

Danielle

$\mathcal{D}$ani stood in her kitchen, watching out the window as Benji and his team started to rebuild the barn. He'd spent the past two weeks clearing the charred remains. They had already dug out the ground for the foundation—bigger and deeper than before—and they were progressing at a rapid pace.

There was a lot of them there today, Miller people, that is. She counted seven in total. Normally she would be out there, either working with the rest of them or doing other tasks around the farm where she wouldn't be in their way, but she was maybe, sorta, kinda avoiding Benji.

It'd been two days since the forest fire drama, and she was still pretty embarrassed by her actions. And also confused. And also, _far_ too curious about him for her own good.

It wasn't her fault! Although her memories were fuzzy, she could recall how he looked that night, all heroic and kind as he helped her haul those sandbags to the fire.

He could have told her she was being crazy. He could have told her that she was being ridiculous. But he hadn't. He had backed her up even when her parents thought she was cuckoo.

He didn't have to do that, and she couldn't figure out why he did, so she settled on watching him until she could puzzle it out.

He clambered out of one of the heavy pieces of machinery they had driven over from the Miller Ranch and walked over to the water truck. She tried to catch his mouth movement as he talked to what she guessed was his foreman for the day. She was terrible at reading lips though.

She sipped at her water, sure that he was going to get right back into the equipment, but instead he hopped over to the pretty horse he brought around every so often. With an ease that could only come from years of riding, he swung his long, lanky legs onto the horse and took off at a gentle trot.

He quickly passed beyond her vision, around toward the front of the house. For a moment she heaved a sigh, telling herself to stop being some creepy McStalker just because someone was acting weird, but then she decided the front garden could do to be watered.

Different from their vegetable garden, which was a joint project between her and her mother, the front yard was almost all Mrs. Touhey. There were flowers upon flowers upon flowers, all different kinds, all different colors, and punctuated by beautiful morning glory vines crawling up the sunny side of their house. Ma made sure to carefully groom them on trellises around the windows, so all in all, it made quite the pretty sight.

When she was younger, Dani had outright refused to have anything to do with the flower garden, mistakenly believing it would ruin her tomboy image and that girly things were stupid. Thankfully, she'd learned quite a bit since then.

She grabbed the hose from the front of the house—Pa had been sure to set up multiple spigots around the house to make sure any greenery would always be within range of water. Apparently, back before Dani was born, her Mom would patiently take bucket after bucket from the well until all of her plants were properly hydrated.

Dani couldn't imagine that. The garden sprawled all the way out to their drive, spanning nearly half of their house in length and just as wide.

After grabbing the hose and starting in the farthest corner, she could still see Benji out of the corner of her eye. He was taking a walk around the entire perimeter of things on his horse, for all the world looking like something out of a spaghetti western.

Dani could see it now; he'd be quite the leading man. All crooked smile and charming words. Looking at her in the morning light like—

She shook her head.

She was *not* thinking nice and crush-like things about *Benji Miller.* How cliché would that be? The high school fat girl and social reject having a crush on the popular boy.

Except... Benji wasn't acting like how popular boys were supposed to act. He was acting like a decent human being, and that was throwing her off. Could it be that she was wrong about him?

She spent an extra-long time making sure the garden was *really* watered, but eventually it got conspicuous. Besides, it was about lunchtime and she could see all the workers beginning to take a break for lunch, which meant they sat in the shade of the one weeping willow they had on the property and ate the boxed lunches that looked far too delicious and well-made to be actual boxed lunches.

Well, she was sure there would be nothing quite like a delicious glass of cool lemonade to go with their meal.

She didn't question herself as she wound the hose back up and went to the kitchen, pulling out their juicer to grind some lemons. But first, she placed them in the microwave for about ten seconds. Most people didn't know it but heating up citrus first gets a whole lot more liquid out of it.

It didn't take her long to then cut the lemons in half and drain all the juice from them. Then it was just some added sugar and a little tiny splash of grapefruit juice. She didn't add water, instead choosing to add two entire trays' worth of ice cubes. They would melt in the warm liquid and cool it down at the same time.

Stirring it all up, she checked to make sure there was enough water in it. Sometimes the ice didn't melt nearly as much as she wanted.

Yeah, still a little *too* tart. She added a tiny bit more water then tasted it again.

There. Tangy but sweet. Perfect.

She knew that it was silly for her to care so much about a silly summer drink, but she couldn't help it. Ever since that morning, waking up with Benji looking at her after a night of basically putting up with her being almost insane, she couldn't get him out of her head.

It was like back when one of the church girls had gotten her a ten-thousand-piece puzzle of a rainbow as a joke. It was meant to be unenjoyable, but she'd gotten obsessed with it, working at it every night until she solved the entire thing.

Granted, it had taken three weeks, but she had done it, and definitely had a fun time. Not to mention the satisfaction when the whole thing was laid out in front of her, all sparkling and perfect.

She'd been so proud, in fact, that she'd lacquered it and hung it up in her room, where it still hung framed over her door.

Grabbing an entire sleeve of plastic cups that they used whenever it was their turn to pitch in at the church's after-service bagel spread, she hoisted the pitcher with her free hand and headed out.

She strode across the lawn and right up to the men, trying to act like this was something she would normally do. Considering they all stopped and stared at her in surprise, she guessed that she wasn't too successful.

Then again, it could just be that she was directly addressing them. In all the days they had been there, she'd always tried to avoid them at all costs.

"Oh, hey there, Dani," Benji said, getting to his feet. His eyes went right to the pitcher in her arms, condensation drizzling down it. "That for us?"

"Yeah. Thought you guys might be thirsty."

"We might be," he said, looking down at the ground and then up through his lashes. *Goodness*, that was a killer look if she had ever seen one.

"You didn't have to do that," he said.

"It's just lemonade," she rebuffed automatically, mentally kicking herself as she did. If she wanted to figure this guy out, then she needed to not have all her walls and weapons right out at first bat.

That was so hard. He was tied to a whole lot of bad memories, even if it was kinda indirectly.

"Well still, that's mighty sweet of you."

"Actually, it's a bit sour."

It took a lot of willpower not to chuckle at her especially terrible pun, keeping a straight face as he looked her over in surprise.

"Did you just tell a joke?"

"Maybe," she said with a shrug. "So, you guys gonna take this, or you gonna make me stand here and hold it forever..."

That seemed to jolt the men and they quickly stood, one taking the pitcher from her and another taking the cups to hand out. Soon everyone had a drink in their hand and a chorus of appreciative sounds issued around her.

She watched Benji perhaps a little too intently as he gulped the drink down. He'd already had her lemonade before, but not fresh, and it was quite satisfying to see his eyes widen in appreciation.

"*Man*, that's good," he said when his glass was empty.

Wow, he really had liked it. He had downed the entire thing in one go.

"You're welcome," she said with a grin. "Make sure y'all recycle the cups over in the bin, okay?" And with that she headed off, hands in her pockets.

"Wait, aren't you gonna have some?"

Dani shook her head. "I actually don't like much but water and the occasional coffee."

"But you—"

She shrugged. "Hey, I've got to have some sort of skill to make up for all the spikes in my personality."

And with that she walked off. Sure, she wanted to figure this Benji guy out more, but she didn't want him to know that's what she was doing.

Granted, as soon as she was inside, she went back to the kitchen and resumed her watching.

Goodness, she really was being a creeper.

She didn't even want to know how long she stood there, but thankfully she heard her mom coming in before the matriarch could catch her mooning out the kitchen window at the man who was helping her family so much.

"Oh hey, Ma, what'cha got there?"

Her mother was carrying several bags. Nothing too heavy, but in Dani's opinion, her mother had done enough hard work already in her life and shouldn't have to break a sweat for anything but her flowers.

"Apparently, that lovely Mrs. Miller organized a charity drive in town since we're waiting on the insurance money a bit longer than we thought we would have to. She completely surprised Pa and me with it when we went into town for groceries."

"Huh, those Millers really don't quit, do they?" Dani said, shaking her head. "Just please tell me it isn't more casseroles."

They had tried their hardest not to waste a single drop of food given to them after the first fire, even freezing whatever they could, but in the end, their fridge stuffed with casseroles had been too much for them, and they'd had to throw away several dishes. If Dani's brothers were around, they would have been able to clean it out no problem.

But if Dani's brothers were around, then they wouldn't need all the charity, would they?

That thought rankled her, and she pushed it out of her mind as her mother responded.

"No, no casserole. But there's plenty of toilet paper, soap, and fresh vegetables, and even gift cards. She really went above and beyond." Mom set the bags on the table and gave Dani an earnest look. "You know, I'm very well aware that we haven't had the best relationship with them in the past, but I don't know what we'd be doing without them right now."

Tears prickled at the corner of her mom's eyes and Dani pulled her into a hug.

"Oh, hey there. It's okay. They really have done a lot for us."

"It's just... I'm so grateful. And I don't know what to do about that. It's like there's so much bad in our lives right now that sometimes it feels like they're the one beacon of good. Like I can trust them. I haven't felt like that about anyone outside of this family for a long time."

"I know what you mean, Mom." Emotions welled up in her stomach. "They really have made a difference, haven't they?"

She nodded, then pulled away, wiping at her eyes. "Do you want to go help your father with the rest of the bags? It's quite a lot. I think even between the two of you it'll take a couple trips."

Dani was all ready to say yes, but then something stopped her. Looking back out the window, she felt another flood of strange emotions as she saw Benji walking back toward his equipment.

"Actually, give me like five minutes. I gotta do something first."

"Oh?" Mom asked. "And what's that?"

"You'll see," she said, giving her mom a sly smile. "I think I'm about to do something crazy."

Before her mom could ask her anything else, she was out the door and crossing the grounds yet again. She reached Benji right as he was about to start up whatever machine he was using, and she waved to catch his attention before she lost her nerve.

He took his safety glasses off, and then earplugs, giving her a surprised look. "Uh, what's up? More lemonade?"

"No," Dani answered before taking a deep breath. A *very* deep breath. Possibly the deepest breath she could have ever taken. "Actually, I wanted to ask you out."

It didn't seem possible, but his big and dreamy eyes went wider.

"You what?"

Oh goodness. She hadn't misread things, had she? Had she suddenly made things weird with a guy who was just trying to help her family?

But she had to finish what she started. She was stubborn like that.

"I wanted to know if you wanted to go out with me. Like to dinner. Or a movie. Or something. As a thank-you," she added on with only the tiniest bit of a wince.

She had never really been known for her smoothness, but she was really botching things.

He was still looking at her like she was a three-headed monster from outer space. "You... want to go... out with me?"

"Yeah." Geez, she could feel her cheeks burning. "Unless you don't want to. And don't feel pressured. I just wanna show you, uh, my gratitude. For, you know, everything that you and your family have done for us."

He continued to stare at her, and for a moment, she was right back in high school, trying to have a social interaction that was completely out of her depth. Just when she thought she was going to literally melt from her embarrassment, Benji swallowed then gave her a slow nod.

"Sure, that sounds like it'd be nice."

13

———

Benji

Benji paced nervously around the family room area of his bachelor's cabin, practically wearing a hole in the floor but not really caring. It wasn't like he had his boots on inside. If there was one thing Ma had drilled into him, it was that shoes were for outdoors, not indoors.

He couldn't believe it. When Dani had marched up to him, all purpose and agitation, he had expected a sort of dressing down for staring at her so often. But it wasn't like he could help it. Ever since that night, watching her sleep and seeing all the worry and weight that etched into her features even when she was unconscious, he couldn't get her out of his head. He wanted to comfort her. To make things better.

He also wanted to get to know the smiling, laughing girl he saw in the grocery store. The woman behind all those defenses.

So yeah, he'd taken a couple of looks at her. Or maybe a couple dozen. Who was keeping track? It wasn't his fault that she was suddenly around a whole lot more, appearing in the corners of his vision like a magnet.

Wait... what had gotten him on his tangent?

Oh right.

She'd asked *him* out.

It was about the last thing he had expected, and Benji groaned at the memory of how he had just stared at her like an utter buffoon. It was like there was a delay between his ears and his brain, trying to decipher the impossible words coming out of her mouth.

But no, apparently that all had been real, and he'd finally managed to fumble out a response.

He had a date with Dani Touhey.

He'd been floating on a cloud in the two days since, surprised at how excited he was. He hadn't been on a date in years, mostly because it was a lot of work and seemed like a waste of both time and energy, but he found his attitude doing a quick one-eighty on that.

Except, now that his date was only two hours away, nerves had replaced every single positive emotion he'd had.

What if this went like the first time they met? What if he said something really stupid and she never wanted to talk to him again? What if this was her convoluted and polite way to tell him that she appreciated his help, but he needed to stop mooning over her at her family ranch?

Well... then he would. It would suck, that was for certain, but he would respect her wishes. Sure, it would be difficult, especially since he was so weirdly caught up with getting to know the real her, but that wouldn't matter. If he made her uncomfortable, then he made her uncomfortable, and he would respect that.

God, he hoped he wasn't making her uncomfortable.

He grabbed his phone from where it was sitting on his small kitchen counter and checked the time. If he left now, he'd get there a half hour early and that would be... not great. He needed to kill at least twenty minutes, preferably not pacing holes in his own floor.

"Come on, Benji. Get it together."

Rubbing his face in his hands, he grabbed his suit jacket and headed out the door. He was going for a mix between fancy and casual, with nice pants, a plain T-shirt, and then a single-breasted suit-jacket on top of it. He normally never cared about his clothing. It was just something that his Ma had ordered from a catalog and eventually made its way into his closet. But he found himself wanting to impress Dani.

Which was pretty silly. She seemed to be the type of person who was the least swayed by things like designer clothes and nice cars and riches. In fact, it usually seemed to turn her off.

Not that he was looking to turn her on, or anything. It was just, he was... he wanted to make sure she knew that he put effort into it. Because she was worth the effort. A date with her was—

"Hey, you okay there? You look like you're about to have an apoplexy."

Benji looked up to realize that he had already gotten to the main house and was standing in the door with his shoes still on. Bart was lounging in the doorway that led to the kitchen, drinking a soda. Where he had gotten that to drink, Benji didn't know, because Ma refused to buy such sugary treats and his older brother never went to town on his own.

"Where did you get contraband caffeine from?" he asked, trying to sound cool.

But his muscled brother shook his head and laughed. "Uh-uh. No changing the subject. What's with the face?"

"This face?" Benji asked playfully. "You mean the one I was born with? The one that has the same DNA makeup as you?"

Bart drained his soda and tucked the bottle under his arm. He knew better than to throw it out where Ma would find it.

"Huh, I ain't seen you this worked up since Tabitha needed surgery when you were a teen. What's going on? Normally you're about as cool as a cucumber."

"Hey, Tabitha was one of the best cows we had, and I—"

"Changing the subject again."

Bart crossed over to Benji and clapped him on the shoulder. While he was happy to see his veteran of a brother acting like a normal human being, Benji had gotten used to the foggy-eyed state the large man used to wander around in. It was strange to have him be so lucid and picking up on anything emotional.

"Come on, brother. I know I've been weird, but you can talk to me if you need to." His face morphed into a sort of wistful smile that Benji had never seen before. "I've learned a lot about talking about things from Missy. I'm getting better at it."

Benji saw his chance to get the attention off himself and went for it. Although he mentally complained about his middle child syndrome, he wasn't sure he was comfortable with all the intense attention from the second oldest of his brothers.

"Oh yeah, how is she doing?"

Bart's smile went even wider. "Man, *so* well. She's back on muck-raking and everyone in the barn loves her. She's been saving up a lot of money and is thinking of opening her own rescue in town. Apparently, a lot of people will get hamsters or rabbits and not know how care-intensive those animals are, and her apartment is getting too full. She's also thinking of holding classes to help educa—*Wait a minute!*" His eyes sharpened and he gave Benji a reproachful look. "You did it again."

Benji snickered and ducked the playful punch his brother threw. "All right. You win. If even Missy can't distract you, then you're not gonna let go."

"You got that right."

"I have a date."

Bart's eyebrows practically shot all the way up to his hairline.

"Come on, it's not *that* surprising," Benji said.

"Benji, no offense, but I don't think I've ever seen you show interest in a woman since I shipped off. And even in high school, you seemed to mostly just like flirting with them and playing with their hair."

"It was *braiding* their hair, and I liked the way it smelled, and doing something with my hands made me less nervous."

"*Uh-huh.* That still doesn't address the whole woman thing. I guess I assumed you were too chill to ever really care about anything like that."

"I mean... that's how I usually am. But with this girl, er, *woman*, it's different."

"Different how?"

Benji shrugged, feeling a bit put on-the-spot. "I don't know. Different. I can tell she doesn't give two beans about our money. And she's impossibly strong and determined. I mean... you remember when there was a tornado when we were real young, and we had to go to the cellar with all our cousins?"

Bart nodded, his expression open and engaged. Huh, Missy really had been working with him on his listening.

"Yeah, I remember that."

"Well, she's like that."

"A tornado?"

Benji shifted from foot to foot, feeling like his words weren't doing her justice. He was the fixer guy, the guy who got along with everyone, not a darn poet.

"Yeah."

"...and her being a tornado makes you want to date her?"

A groan sounded from between his lips. "You're making it sound terrible! When I say a tornado, it's not that she's destructive or kills people like a literal pillar of wind. I just mean it as in... well, she seems unstoppable. Like she'd fling anyone who dared stop her far, far away. There's this, I dunno, *inevitability* to her that just draws me in. And I feel like..."

Oh boy, he hadn't come into this conversation expecting to try to articulate why he couldn't get the woman out of his head, but he was giving it his best shot.

"I feel like if I can make it through those winds, and that bluster, that there'll be this perfect calm in the center of it, and that's right where I want to be."

To his surprise, Bart smiled again. It wasn't quite as love-sick as his first grin, but it was quite proud.

"I don't think I've ever seen you try so hard to describe anything in your entire life."

Benji felt himself blush at that. "Yeah, well it's important to me. I mean, I'd like it if *she'd* be important to me."

Another supportive pat from his brother that felt more like a slap. Benji was pretty hardened from ranch life, but *geez* his brother was *big*. He'd clearly been hogging all the Thor-genes that were running through their heritage.

"Only one way to find out if she will. What time's the date?"

Benji looked at his phone. "Huh, I actually should head out about now."

"What'd you stop by here for if it was time to go already?"

"I came by to distract myself from feeling nervous. So, thanks. Your need to make this whole thing incredibly awkward was actually useful."

Bart chuckled. "Well, you know me, I live to serve."

"That's about right." Benji looked over his brother, taking him in from head to foot. Of course, the veteran was still undergoing treatment, but it was like he actually had his brother back. It was nice. "And I'm glad. You know that, right?"

"Huh, glad for what?"

"That you lived."

A soft, unguarded expression crossed the man's face. "You know what? Me too."

It was entirely unplanned, but the two of them both leaned in for a hug. Benji felt his chest squeeze a bit, knowing that Dani would probably give anything to hug her injured brothers like he was right now.

Far too many times he had been forced to think about what it would be like to lose Bart. Now that the military man was safe at home, he wanted Dani to feel that same sort of solace. He wished he could march to the hospital and cure the two men he'd never met, but that was well out of his power.

The two pulled away and Benji gave his brother a solid nod then headed out the door. Actions often spoke louder than words, so that hug said everything much better than he ever could.

BENJI PULLED UP, parking in the drive and walking up to the front door. If he was younger, he would have asked permission from the parents to take their daughter out—parents had always loved that—but he figured that Dani was a grown woman and wouldn't appreciate that in the slightest.

So instead he settled on texting her that he was there while he walked up to the door. That way she'd have a little extra warning to put her shoes on and look in the mirror one last time. Although he couldn't really imagine confident, prickly Dani giving two flying flips what he thought of her. In fact, he wouldn't be surprised if she answered the door in her over—

The door opened, and his thoughts cut off as he realized who was standing there, looking up at him with the same uncertainty he was feeling.

It was Dani, of course. But it also was so completely *not* Dani that he could only stare at her for several solid moments. Her hair was loose from its always-present braid or ponytail, falling around her head and shoulders in soft waves. It was much longer than he ever thought it was, falling just to the neckline of the dress she was wearing.

That *dress.*

It was the prettiest shade of peach he had ever seen, cut close to her body on top and then flaring out in the rockabilly style. It hugged her body like a revelation, and he could see black stockings on her thick, shapely legs to match the lacey shrug over her muscled arms. Or were they thigh highs? He supposed there was only one way to find out...

"You're here right on the dot," she said.

Thankfully she interrupted his thoughts before they went somewhere they very much should not go. Especially not on a first date. It was only then he noticed she was wearing makeup. Lipstick, mascara, whatever it was that women did to make themselves look like God was shining a spotlight on one of his favorite creations. It was a simple, beautiful effect that he guessed probably was anything but simple to do.

Wow, she looked beautiful. All done up like a present and just for him. It made his blood rush through his body, and he coughed to cover his shocked reaction.

He didn't think it worked.

"You look lovely," he said, keeping his eyes on her pretty face and not swooping lower to the lacey, delicate neckline of the dress she was wearing. But Lord on High, it certainly was a temptation. They didn't build women like her as often anymore. Or if they did, the world shamed them so much that they hid away, swaddled under too many layers.

It really was a sad state of affairs. Because the only thing that was more beautiful than a woman like Dani, was a woman who knew exactly what she was worth and loved herself to pieces.

"You are beautiful," he managed to sputter, feeling like an absolute fool.

He was normally so funny, but all he felt like he could do was point and say things like he was a Cro-Magnon. You Woman. Smell good. We go food? Ugh. How embarrassing.

"Thanks," she said, lifting her chin and squaring her shoulders in that way he liked.

Whenever she did it, he always felt like she was about to march off to battle.

"I figured since you were gracious enough to give me your time, I might as well doll myself up a bit."

"Oh, well, you're a doll no matter what you're wearing."

Wait. Had he really said that? What was *wrong* with him? He was twenty-seven years old, not a sixty-year-old man!

But to his surprise, Dani flushed at that. "Well, I don't think I've ever seen a doll that's built like me but thank you."

That's because you're one of a kind.

He just barely resisted saying the cheesy line and instead offered her his arm.

"Shall we?"

They had agreed to go to dinner together. It allowed for more talking than a movie, and there was a nice diner in town.

Granted, it was the only diner in town, but that was all right by him. With his Ma's good home cooking, they rarely went out, so he'd never gotten a chance to get tired of the greasy-spoon fair like most of the other locals.

He walked her to his truck, only letting go of her to open her door. He missed the contact instantly. Her hand was so soft, and she smelled like citrus. If he didn't know better, he would think that she was made specifically to attract every part of him.

But that would be selfish. And he wasn't selfish.

...even if she made him want to be a little selfish.

Once she was comfortably inside, he shut the door and crossed around to the driver's side. It felt like his heart was beating a million miles a minute as he got in beside her and turned on the ignition.

His radio blared loud, startling the both of them, and she let out the cutest yelp before he could reach over and shut it off. Flushing a bit, he gave her what he hoped was a charming smile.

"Sorry about that. I drove over with my windows down."

"That's all right," she said, hand over her heart. "I like to do that same thing. Granted, usually when I'm not so done up. It takes a whole lot of effort to make me look this presentable for public interaction."

"I bet," he agreed, flattered that she had even tried at all for just a silly date with him.

But then he realized *what* he was agreeing with and quickly tried to backpedal.

"I mean, not that it would take a great deal of effort to make you look presentable. I'm just saying I guess I could understand it being inconvenient to get yourself into a dress and hosiery and—"

"Relax," she said with a low chuckle. "And you're right. Pantyhose are always a pain so I never wear them. These are stockings I got on clearance online. They have a faux garter belt attached to them so I don't have to worry about them rolling down, and my legs are short enough that I don't get thigh rub."

She said it all so frankly, and Benji just focused his whole mind on driving into town and not exactly what thigh highs with attached garters might look like on her generous figure.

"Oh. I didn't know that was a thing."

"Me either, until I found them. I tell you, I don't know what fat women did before the internet. I love several plus size shops they have in the city, but we don't have a single one in our town."

"You're not fat," Benji retorted instantly. He didn't even think on that one.

"What? But I am."

He opened his mouth to object further. He didn't like her saying anything negative about herself when she basically looked like an enchanting and dangerous siren sitting right there next to him.

"You know, fat isn't a *bad* thing. Or even a bad word. It's just a descriptor. Just like someone might say you're tall, or lanky, or have a nice face. I'm short, fat, and I have pretty great lips."

She *did* have pretty great lips. Lips that he was very much not looking at while he watched the road.

"People treat it like an insult, or that it's shameful, but it's not. It's just an adjective like any other. If people could just realize that and move on with their lives, well everyone would be a whole lot happier."

"Fair enough," Benji said with a nod as he thought it over.

He knew that the world liked to shame fat people, from concern over their health to discrimination with jobs and all of that, but he never really thought of the how, why or much else about it. He guessed there was a lot of negative connotations tied up in there that didn't need to be. Fat was just that. Fat. Neither good nor bad nor really having any morality at all.

"You look like you're thinking," Dani said in amusement beside him.

"Of course, I am. You said something worth thinking about."

He caught her flush out of the corner of his eye. "Usually when I start talking about fat-phobia or anything social, people zone out."

"That's because a lot of people don't like to challenge things they assume are true."

"Oh, and you do?"

Benji shrugged. "I dunno. If I think a barn is in good shape, but then a professional carpenter comes along and tells me the beams are made wrong, I feel like I should at least take what he says into consideration and do my research. Sure, it may be uncomfortable and annoying that I gotta do all this extra work, but if it resulted in a better barn, I really have no room to complain."

She chuckled lightly. The sound was so perfect that he resolved to make her do it again and again.

She was smiling. "Not a perfect metaphor, but I get it. And thank you. Even my brothers will just try to change the subject."

"They don't agree with you?"

"Nah, they just find that societal talk boring. They don't see the need to worry about what's outside our door when we all have each other."

"But you think differently?"

"Well, yeah. Just look at the situation we're in now. I could lose them any day now and then it'll just be my folks and me."

That soured the mood considerably, and Benji watched her expression go from playful to incredibly guilty. It was like seeing her shrink in real time and he was reminded of that terribly wounded conversation in the grocery store.

"It's not your fault, you know."

"Hmm?" she said, turning her whole upper body toward the window. Although Benji couldn't see her reflection, he didn't need it to know that she was tearing up. He could hear it in her voice.

"Your brothers. It's not your fault. They're grown men and, although I don't really know them yet, I'm willing to bet that they're just as stubborn as you are."

That got a shaky laugh out of her. "Oh, so you think I'm stubborn?"

"Hey you, don't turn this around on me. I was *trying* to comfort you," he joked. He liked joking. It was what he was good at, not all this emotional mumbo jumbo.

"I know," she murmured, finally turning back to face the front. "And thanks."

"Any time, ma'am."

"Ew. Don't call me ma'am. Like, ever. Especially since I'm a year younger than you."

"What, you don't like my dashing cowboy role-play?"

"Oh, role-play on the first date? That's pretty forward for this town."

Benji felt his heart thunder at her casual joke. She said it so matter-of-factly, giving him a lopsided grin, and he couldn't help but wonder who this woman was. He preferred coasting through life, enjoying everything and never getting too ruffled up. Working on the farm and hanging out with his brothers and family. No stress. No problems that usually weren't solved in a day or two.

But Dani. Dani made him want to experience *more*. She so fearlessly grabbed life by the reins and did whatever she wanted, seeing the worst in people but never stopping. She was like a live wire, and he wanted to grasp it with both hands just to see how it felt.

Huh, he wondered if maybe he should stop comparing her to dangerous, harmful things.

Or just things in general, because she was a human being. Possibly the most human one he'd ever met outside of his family.

"What's the matter?" she persisted when he had fallen silent. "Cat got your tongue?"

"Nah, it's just anything I think of saying doesn't seem like something polite you should say to a lady."

She snorted, and it was strangely cute. Just like everything about her.

"I ain't a lady."

"Coulda fooled me. You seem to have the uniform on."

"Please, being a lady is a way of life, not a wardrobe, and one I reject outright."

"Then what are you?" Benji asked, thoroughly amused.

He liked how Dani could effortlessly churn from one bit of wit to the other, never trying to placate him or figure out what she needed to say to endear herself to him. She was just so effortlessly *her*. Either take her or leave her.

And Benji certainly didn't want to leave her.

"I'm..." She seemed to think it over for a moment, as if she was surprised that Benji was continuing the conversation. He wondered if other people had shut her down in the past. "I'm Dani. And that's enough."

"Yes," Benji agreed wholeheartedly. "It certainly is."

14

———

Benji

*B*enji pulled into a parking spot at the cozy diner, throwing his truck into park before sliding out and rushing around to open Dani's door for her. Just as he guessed, she hadn't been expecting that and already was moving to get out.

"Oh, right..." she said as he held his hand out to her. "Figures you'd be old-fashioned."

"Treating your date respectably is not old-fashioned," Benji countered. "Besides, of the two of us, who is wearing high heels and has to jump down from my truck?"

"Hah! You may have a point there." Her hand rested on his arm as she did indeed jump to the ground, but she did it without so much as a wobble. She was quite sturdy for being in a pair of demure black... what kind of shoes were those? He had bought a pair once for a cousin on the ranch his age as a birthday present, but really his mother had picked them out.

Wedges. That was right. He remembered something about the sole gave women more... stability? Or something? He didn't know. Women's fashions were weird and uncomfortable, but boy did he like how they made Dani's legs look.

"All right, shall we go inside?"

He picked up on the fact that she sounded nervous but was nice enough to ignore it. He'd been around Dani enough to know that appearing unruffled and strong was a safety measure for her, and he had no desire to weaken the façade if she was feeling antsy.

Besides, he could guess what was bothering her given what he knew of her history. Apparently, she'd been mercilessly mocked in high school for her weight, clothes and just not being a Miller in general but daring to be the child of ranchers. He imagined showing up on the arm of an actual Miller's son was going to cause plenty of talk.

But it was to be expected. Ever since Ben had gotten back together with Chastity and married her, the whole town had been abuzz with their most sought-after bachelors going off the market. Then, when Bart and Missy became more well-known as a couple, people *really* started giving the three remaining brothers the eye.

Bryant had certainly taken advantage of that, shacking up with plenty of girls who had dreams of marrying into the wealth, but he would always break it off with them before a week could even pass.

But Benji had taken all of this into consideration. At first, he had intended to go far away to the city, where they could have a great date away from prying eyes. But then he realized that he *wanted* people to see him and Dani together. That maybe they'd get a glimpse of the amazing things he saw in her and give her a break. Maybe be a bit friendlier.

Or maybe he just wanted to show her off. Like some sort of weird, middle-child need to declare that he was interested in someone before anyone else could swoop by and snap her up.

His mind was brought back to the present and the actual date rather than the *why* of how he had planned it. Holding the door open for Dani, they then walked over to the hostess, who greeted them with a classic, customer service smile.

"Two this evening?"

"Yes," Benji said, making sure to put his hand on the small of Dani's back. He wanted it clear that they were here on a date, not as friends or any other excuse that other people might make up in their heads. "A booth please, if you don't mind."

"Of course, right this way."

She grabbed two menus and lead them over to a side booth, letting them both slip in before laying the menus on the table. She said the normal hostess stuff then walked back to her post, and then it was just him and Dani.

On their date.

He almost couldn't believe it was happening. Sitting in front of him, bathed in the old lights of the diner, she looked like a classic movie star captured in soft filter, all smooth edges and femininity.

"What?" she asked when he'd been gazing at her just a little too long. "It's too soon for me to have something in my teeth."

"Sorry," he said, propping his chin in his hand. "Just catching up with reality."

"Oh, are you on a three-second delay, or something?"

"You know, it kinda feels like it."

She laughed, shaking her head and making her hair bounce all around. He wished he could feel it in his hands but reaching over and grasping a copper strand seemed entirely too forward.

Dani tilted her head and a mischievous look came to her eyes. "You've found my secret. I'm actually an ancient deity and my sheer amount of gravitas can warp the perception of time around me."

He couldn't stop the laugh before it was out of his mouth. Not that he would want to stop it. "Funny, I always thought it was gravity that did that."

"Close enough."

Benji opened his mouth to respond, but he was startled by the waitress as she seemed to pop out of thin air beside them.

"Hi, there! My name is Rachel, and I'll be your server. Well I'll be, Dani Banani, is that you?"

Benji's eyes flicked to Dani just in time to see all of the color drain from her face. "Rachel. Hi."

Wait. Rachel? Benji felt like he knew that name. Rachel... *Rachel.*

"And double goodness gracious! Is that *Benji Miller*? What are you doing here? I swear I ain't seen ya off the ranch since two or three years ago."

Right then the barest hint of a memory slid into place. She had been a cheerleader... With dark, pretty hair who liked double French braids and would always bring him beef jerky for his troubles. That seemed right.

"I go to church sometimes," he said as politely as he could. Which probably wasn't actually very polite, but he wanted to get back to his date with Dani, who was looking more and more uncomfortable by the second.

"Of course, you do, you Miller sons are all such good people. Our town is lucky to have you." Her smile grew saccharine sweet. "Lookey here, even doing charity with my little Dani Banani here. That's so kind of you, considering all that happened with that terrible fire."

"I'm not your Dani Banani."

"It's not charity."

Both Benji and Dani spoke at the same time, her tone heated and his urgent, but Rachel just blithely went on to take their drink order. Benji was wondering if her unintentional barb was maybe a little intentional, but before he could decide one way or another, she was whisking off.

Benji looked to Dani, who had that same stone face on that she had been wearing when he had first met her.

"Are you okay?" he asked quickly. "I can ask for a new waitress. Or we can go."

"No!" she objected emphatically before blushing. "I mean, no. One, the things that happened between me and her were in high school. Now that I've... been through what I've been through, they really don't seem all that important. Two, if I leave, it shows her that she still has power over me. And she doesn't."

Dani drew in a deep breath, and he felt some of her previous good mood recover.

"So no. I'd like to stay here with you and enjoy this date and your company."

He decided to turn the tables on her with the same teasing she'd done earlier.

"Oh, so you enjoy my company then?"

To his surprise, she didn't backtrack or sputter or banter back. Instead, she gave a sharp nod. "Yes."

Oh.

Well then.

"Glad to be of service," was all he could say, wishing he had his drink just to have something to do while his brain thought of what to say next.

There was a lull in the conversation for a moment, but it wasn't an awkward one. If anything, it was the opposite of that. Dani was gazing at the table, a contented, almost thoughtful expression on her face, and that gave Benji another chance to look over her again.

She really was something. All cherub-faced and innocent-looking, but with the strength of iron just underneath. She would have been a great spy back in the day. Letting people underestimate her and then ripping the rug right out from under them.

Then again, she seemed to have people constantly underestimating her already. Including him when he had first met her. He was glad he had gotten wise to that before she did any rug-pulling on him.

The comfortable silence was broken as Rachel showed up with their drinks, pulling a little notepad from her apron.

"Do you two folks know what you'd like to order?"

Well, at least that was one thing Benji knew he could do without somehow looking the fool.

"Yeah, actually. I'd like your open-faced burger, with extra mac and cheese on top. Mashed potatoes on the side, extra gravy."

She laughed too loudly and brightly, making him almost wince. He caught himself at the last second, but it wasn't the easiest feat.

"Well look at you! I guess with all that muscle and hard ranch work, you really bust up an appetite, don't you?"

"Uh, yeah..."

"Goodness, if I ate half of that, it would go right to my hips!"

"Uh-huh."

Benji didn't know how to comment on that. Rachel would be more attractive to him if she did add a little bit to her very tiny hips, but he didn't believe she should change her body to fit his preference. He also thought it would be pretty rude to indicate that she wasn't his type right out in the open while she was working.

Thankfully, she moved on to Dani.

"And for you, Ms. Banani?"

"It's Dani. And I think I'll do the biscuits and gravy."

"Oh, honey! You haven't been here in a while, but did ya see we got salads now? They're pretty good. I'm in love with the strawberry and avocado spinach salad."

Something about her tone was off, and Benji lifted his gaze from where he had been scoping out the desserts. He got the feeling that something was happening right in front of him, but he didn't know what.

But... it was weird that Rachel would suggest a salad, right? That had to be weird.

"Oh yeah, I've had the salads here before, but I want something more filling since I've had a long day. Biscuits and gravy, please."

"Just trying to watch out for ya, girl. All those carbs, ya know? And it's so late in the day."

Wait. Now he knew things weren't right.

"Rachel," he started, but then Dani was cutting him off.

"I am so impressed that you're continuing your study of nutrition while waitressing full time, but I assure you, I know what I'd like to eat tonight."

"All right then girlie. Li'l Dani here always did love her pizza!" Another laugh that he liked even less than her last one. "I remember all the time she'd go up for seconds at the cafeteria. Sometimes she'd even polish off ours at the table if we were full. You know, since we were all watching our figures for cheerleading."

To Benji's great horror, she reached down and gently pinched Dani's cheek. "You're still our chubby-faced little kitten, aren't you?"

Benji reached out and pulled her hand away, setting it down at her side. "I think you should go get our order."

"Huh?" Her smile curled wickedly, and suddenly Benji got the sense that he was looking at a cat who had just managed to eat the canary. "I was just reminiscing. You know, 'cause she was a cutie."

He had been a little slow on the uptake, but he could tell that she meant the exact opposite.

"She *is*. As in present tense. And I would call her beautiful, not cute, but I understand it's different between girlfriends." He let enough tone seep into his voice to let her know that he was wise to her games. To be perfectly honest, he was having a difficult time containing his temper. It wasn't often that he lost it, but realizing that this woman was trying to humiliate Dani right in front of him made him burn much hotter than he had in years. "I'd appreciate it if you gave our order to another waitress and let us enjoy this date that I've been *very* much looking forward to for several days."

"Y-you—" she sputtered, looking completely shocked at his response. A quick glance to Dani told him that she was regarding him with a similarly surprised expression. "But I—"

"No, no buts. No questions. I think that our interaction is done for the night, Rachel. It's been great reconnecting with you."

He let go of her and tried to give her a charming but empty smile, and thankfully, she seemed to get the message. Letting out a huff, she marched away toward the kitchen.

"I cannot believe you just did that," Dani said with a laugh once the woman was gone.

"I can't believe that you just sat there without knocking her block off," he retorted, feeling embarrassment seep in now that the situation was settling. "She was outright insulting you."

Dani shrugged. "I was handling it. In a way."

"*How?*" he asked, completely baffled.

"I dunno, it's weird, psychological girl code stuff. If I act upset or make a scene, she wins. By playing it cool and always having a comeback, I show that she doesn't phase me. That she's literally nothing to me."

"So what, you two have a fake compliment-off and just progressively hurt each other's feelings until..."

"Until someone interrupts, usually." She sighed. "Look, I know it probably seems strange and passive-aggressive to you, but I can't stand up to most of these people when my family's business relies on us staying just barely out of being social pariahs to this town. If I make her mad, she tells her friends, her friends tell their parents, and the next thing we know, what few contracts we have go to your family, because of course, everyone loves the Millers."

She stopped, her eyes going wide again. "Oh. I'm sorry. I shouldn't have said that."

Benji's mouth twisted a bit. Not because he was angry or hurt, but because he could see the logic behind it. Of course, she had to play a careful game of not pissing off the wrong people but also not being a doormat. The thought of having to live his own life that way made him nauseous. He had no idea that any of that was going on, but now that she pointed it out to him, it seemed obvious.

Was *that* what had been happening all through high school? There'd been intense power struggles and psychological chicanery going on while he'd been braiding hair, kissing girls, and eating way too much junk food for even a teenage boy? No wonder she'd disliked him so much when they had first met.

Well, first *really* met.

"No, it's all right. Look, I know the situation between our families hasn't been the greatest but helping your family has opened my eyes to a lot of stuff. Once your ranch is repaired, I don't want things to go back to how they were."

She smiled, just barely, at that. "I'd like that too."

That made Benji's heart pound. He had been worried that this whole date might have just been her way of making up for their first meeting and only a friendly gesture. Yeah, a *friend* date. But when she said things like that, it made him think that it might be more than that.

He would really, *really* like that.

"Well, glad we're still on the same page."

"Yeah," she agreed. "Usually I'm not even in the same book. Or the same library, for that matter."

"Huh, and here I thought we only had one of those in this town."

"Nah, there's actually a secret library under the town hall that only I know about. But now that I've told you, I'm afraid I'll have to kill you."

Benji laughed at that. When Dani wasn't trying to verbally dress him down, she was pretty hilarious. He felt like he was finally getting to see the woman in the grocery store, and she was just as great as he had thought she'd be.

"And here I thought my inevitable demise would be over who's picking up the check."

She leaned forward at that, her eyes bright and attentive. "Um, as the person who asked you here, clearly I should pay."

"You know, I can see that being a valid line of reasoning. But considering your family has been attacked by an arsonist twice, I think it wouldn't be too much of a stretch for me to cover it."

"But you see, you've helped my family so much, the least *I* can do is cover a meal."

"But having you try to pay me back ruins the point of all my service —" He was cut off as a waitress approached them, this one very much *not* Rachel.

"Opened face burger with extra mac and cheese and mashed potatoes with extra gravy?" she said cheerily.

"That's me," Benji said quickly, eager to get back to the conversation.

The waitress set the heaping plate in front of him, but then slid another, smaller bowl toward him. "We didn't know how much you meant by extra, so I hope this is enough."

Benji looked down at what had to be two servings of mac and cheese on its own then smiled. "It's perfect, thank you."

"Great. Let me know if you need anything else."

Before he could ask where Dani's dish was, a now-familiar voice chorused behind them. "One biscuits and gravy with *extra* gravy!"

It all happened so fast. In one moment, his gaze snapped to Rachel as she approached their table, both of her hands gripping Dani's plate of food. The next second, she seemed to trip over nothing and let that same plate fly. Benji jumped to his feet, trying to warn Dani and push her out of the way at the same time, but he only managed to knock their glasses over.

"Benj—" Dani started to say in surprise, but she never got it out, because then the plate landed over her head, mashing the biscuits into her hair and sending what seemed like a torrent of hot—or at least warm—gravy all down her body.

A shocked, pained cry punched out of her mouth, and Benji strode over to her, trying to pull her shawl from her body. His mother had taught him about coffee burns once, and how they could melt clothes to the body, so he needed to get it off of her fast. That would also have the added bonus of removing a good bit of the gravy, which was quickly soaking into the artificial fibers.

"Oh goodness gracious, I'm so clumsy," Rachel said, sounding entirely pleased with herself.

But Benji didn't even have time to care. He could only see the fabric as he wrested it from Dani's form, and the way the skin along her décolletage and tops of her chest was turning bright pink from the heat. For some reason, Dani was just standing there, panting hard like she couldn't comprehend what was happening.

He just couldn't move his fingers fast enough. People were standing up and walking toward them, and he thought he faintly heard someone ask if they needed help, but none of that mattered. Like a man possessed, he picked Dani right up and carried her to the bathroom. A sink. He needed to get the hot gravy off her. To cool her skin down.

He barely stopped when a hand rested on his chest. His vision clearing, he saw the waitress who had served him his burger standing in front of him, a horrified expression on her face.

"I'll take her into the ladies' room and help her out, okay? This is your first date, right? I'm sure she'd rather you didn't see her like this."

Benji thought of protesting, but then he also remembered that the best thing to do would be to get her out of her dress and her clothes and that was definitely not the job for him. Setting her down quickly, he allowed the waitress to guide her into the bathroom then sank down in the closest chair.

Dani really couldn't catch a break, could she?

"Excuse me, sir?"

Benji looked up from where he'd been holding his head in his hands, trying to quell his rage now that everything was catching up to him, to see an older man dressed in a nice shirt and pants.

"Now's not really the time."

"Yes, sir, I apologize deeply. I'm the owner of this diner. One of my girls called me and said something had happened?"

Well, it looked like some of that anger was getting its chance to rush out.

"What happened is one of your *girls* disapproved of who I was with and was jealous, so she assaulted my date." *Burned her.*

Dear Lord and all his good grace, of all the things that could have happened to Dani, why did it have to be *burning*. She already had so much trauma linked with fire. She didn't need anymore. Benji was briefly reminded of the story of Job from the Bible, and all of his suffering, but he prayed that Dani wasn't about to have to go down a road like *that.*

"I'm sure it wasn't—"

"She insulted my date's weight, teased her, and when I asked for a new waitress, she specifically served Dani and dropped her plate right on her head."

The color of the owner's face drained, and Benji had to remind himself that this man had no idea what the circumstances were.

"I am so, so sorry sir. And your date, where is she now?"

"In the bathroom. One of the servers is helping her clean up. The gravy was hot, so she needed to get it off before it could melt her clothes to her skin or cause any damage to deeper layers of skin."

"*Melt to her—Gott in Hiemmel.* All right, sir. I apologize sincerely. Of course, we will take care of this mess and anything you need. Please, did you happen to catch the name of the server who did this?"

For a brief moment Benji thought about withholding it. About potentially damaging Dani's standing with their small town if he blabbed. But his anger was too hot and his sense of what was right and wrong was demanding justice.

"Rachel," he said with authority. "Her name is Rachel."

"Of course. I will make sure she is dealt with. Please, if there is anything you need, please tell us."

"I will. For starters, you can reimburse the lady for her outfit, which I'm sure is ruined."

"Yes, yes. I'll do that immediately." The owner quickly walked away, returning shortly, handing Benji an envelope filled with cash. "For the lady," he said. The owner walked away again, heading for the kitchen.

The next thing he knew, Benji thought he heard sounds of yelling from the kitchen, but he didn't care. He kept his eyes locked on the bathroom door for what seemed like forever.

It was at least ten minutes later before the waitress came out, looking thoroughly exhausted.

"Hey there," she said, blowing some errant strands out of her face. "She said she needed a few minutes. Thankfully, she doesn't seem to have any burns. But there is skin irritation for sure. Did the owner come by?"

Benji nodded, not trusting his voice at the moment. Where had it all gone wrong? They'd been having such a good time and then...

Chaos.

"If you wanna wait here, I'm sure she'll be out in a bit. Do you want something to drink?"

Benji's first instinct was to say no, but he realized that his mouth felt like sandpaper. "Yeah. A glass of water would be great."

She nodded and headed off, disappearing from his view. He kept his gaze on the door, trying to think of how he was going to make up for this. The whole situation seemed like much more than something a good ice cream or other dessert would fix.

He bristled as his mind turned everything over and over again. Was *this* what Dani had to deal with her entire high school life? How *awful*. How she ended up as a functional human being and not entirely fearful of people was beyond him. He hadn't even been the one who had been spilled on and he felt like breaking something.

Huh. For being considered the most "chill" of all the brothers, he sure was wound up. But he couldn't help it. He wanted to *protect* Dani, not put her into situations where petty people purposefully dumped hot liquids onto her.

He should have been smarter. She had been plenty open about how she didn't have a good relationship with the people of their town, and he hadn't gotten it. And now she had suffered because of it. But he'd wanted everybody to see what he saw. Because if they did, how could they think of her as anything other than the strong, fearless warrior she was.

More minutes ticked by and the waitress returned with a glass of water that he sipped when his stomach wasn't churning. He knew he should ask her name and thank her, then maybe tell the owner how she was one of the good ones, but he couldn't wrench enough of his mind away from the bathroom entrance to do so.

Eventually, at least a half hour had passed, and he was starting to grow concerned. What if she had slipped? Somehow lost consciousness? What if she was in there all alone and he was sitting outside like a buffoon?

He waited a few more moments before finally going to the door, knocking gently as he did. "Hey, Dani, you okay in there?"

There was no response, not even a groan, and alarm shot up inside of him.

"Dani? Can you just make a sound, let me know you're all right?"

Nothing.

He couldn't stand there doing nothing. He *couldn't*. It went against everything in his nature, so he put his hand against the door.

"Dani, I'm gonna come in, okay? I want to warn you, in case you don't want me in, but I'm just making sure you're all right."

Still no response.

That was it. He pushed the door open, half expecting to see her sprawled across the ground or something equally horrific, but instead he was greeted by empty stalls.

"Dani?" he asked, confusion churning through him at the silent room.

She wasn't in there.

She was gone.

But how? He'd been sitting there the whole time! And she didn't even have a car—

A cool breeze drifted across his increasingly hot face, and that was when he noticed the window was open, frosted glass pushed up far enough for someone to definitely go through.

Oh.

The realization hit him with surprising force, clearing the air from his body and stunning him for a moment. It seemed surreal, but he knew as clear as day what had happened.

She had left.

Dani was gone.

15

Danielle

ani stormed up to the front of her house, still in a state of shock from everything that had happened.

The date had been going so well. Little shocks of excitement had been going up her spine, and she had been thoroughly enjoying the conversation. Who had known that Benji could be so funny? Sure, he wasn't as snarky as her, but he rolled with her tangents really well.

People rarely did that. They always found her asides either too distracting or didn't understand. Or they thought she was being preachy. She couldn't help it that she had opinions. She'd had to form them growing up or she would have never survived.

But Benji seemed to think about them. To give them credence or pick up the joke and take it further. It was easy to talk to him. Easy to forget the minutes and just experience things.

Her feet picked up as she almost reached the door. She had used what little extra spending money she had to get the only ride-sharing service in their entire town, but she had them drop her off all the way at the very edge of the drive.

The cool night air helped refresh her. Helped her feel less mortified and soothed the still irritated patches of skin. That gravy had been so *hot.*

She remembered the moment it had first touched her scalp. She'd been staring in surprise at Benji, who had jumped up to his feet and pointed in horror behind her. Then it felt like hot water from the shower was hitting her scalp. Time had picked up after that, dozens of things happening in rapid succession, but all she could do was stand there.

And then he'd *picked her up*.

No one had picked her up since she was eight years old. In any other moment, she would have loved it. Maybe even felt a little flutter of attraction. But all she could feel was the hot, syrupy gravy dripping down her.

She couldn't believe it.

She knew that Rachel was a stone-cold bully, but she'd never expected *that*. Sure, Dani had wanted to haul off and slug her multiple times. She *hadn't* though. Because she knew that physical violence was a line that she should never cross no matter how hurtful the verbal barbs got.

"Oh hey, honey. We didn't even hear the car in the drive. How was your date?" her mom asked from the living room.

"Fine," she answered quickly, running up to her room. She didn't want to answer any questions. She just needed to get away from everything.

She had ruined it.

All of it.

If she had just reacted like a normal human, maybe she could have salvaged the situation. After all, she wasn't the one who had dumped a plate of hot food on someone to get back at them.

But she had frozen like a moron, so badly that Benji had to pick her up and carry her off. And then he'd had to haul a waitress into the bathroom to make sure she didn't let the gravy cook into her own skin.

After the waitress had left, Dani stood there, staring in the mirror. Her skin was bright pink everywhere the gravy had settled, her shrug somewhere else in the restaurant. Her hair still had clumps of meat and biscuits in it.

Ugh. She was such a mess. And that was what he would always see her as. A mess. Because it was when she was staring into the mirror that she realized how stupid she was being. Guys like Benji didn't ever have interest in girls like her. He was rich, successful, handsome and had a great personality. What did she have? Nothing like that. Just a bunch of hang-ups and past trauma.

It was all too much. She felt stupid and alone and entirely like she was smack dab in high school again. Powerless and outmatched by a bunch of girls who had decided that she wasn't worthy of kindness because of her size.

Dani jumped into the shower, trying not to think. She could feel her mind starting to build up into a frenzy again, and she was trying to tramp that down. It wasn't like she'd ever *really* been interested in Benji.

Except she had.

As much as she tried to deny it, as much as she tried to pretend, she wasn't better and smarter than the girls who'd been drooling over him ever since he had hit puberty, she was just the same. All caught up in the charm of him.

Pathetic.

That harsh thought startled her. She thought she'd been better about handling that mean, insidious voice inside of her over the past couple of weeks, but it was suddenly so overpowering. Her breath hitched, and the next thing she knew her eyes were beginning to water.

No.

No.

She wouldn't cry over a boy. Her pride was too great for that.

Finishing washing herself off, she stepped out of the shower and dried herself off before snatching up the first bit of clothing she saw. Running right back down the stairs, she grabbed her keys from the rack by the door.

"Honey, where are you going?"

"I need to see my brothers."

"It's nine o'clock at night!"

But she was already out the door, running over to the old truck her family shared.

She cranked the radio all the way up as she whipped down the drive, as if the music could drown out all of the thoughts churning in her head. Why was she being so childish, so weak, letting her emotions control her so easily? She liked to think she was above it all, but it was so, *so* easy to tear her down.

She pressed the pedal to the metal, speeding along way faster than she normally ever would. But she needed to get to her brothers. Her confidants. Together, the three of them were a unit. Without them, she felt like a firecracker with a lit fuse but no direction to go. She was the passion of the group. The heart. Not the reason.

She arrived in record time, parking in the free lot that was a bit of a walk because she knew that she was going to barely be able to afford the gas back home. But the walk gave her more time to force herself to breathe so that when she showed up at the front desk, she didn't look like she herself needed to be admitted.

Thankfully the nurse on shift recognized her and waved her on. They'd explained to Dani that normally no one was allowed to visit during after-hours, but she could come in for a little while.

Not that she'd visited often. Only four times in three weeks. That definitely wasn't enough. But there was just so much to do on the ranch...

Her thoughts trailed off as she entered her brothers' doorway.

No, she stayed away because seeing them like that reminded her that they were there because of her.

"Hey guys," she murmured quietly, going over to a chair. "Sorry, it's been a while."

She sat down in the same chair she usually did, looking over their faces. She couldn't be sure, but it seemed like they had fewer bandages and more pink, brand-new skin showing. Her parents had mentioned that the doctors were talking about waking them up, but they wanted to be sure they were ready to come off the ventilators first.

"You know, a lot's been going on with me. Crazy stuff. I don't even know if you'd believe it." She paused, as if they would magically wake up and respond. They didn't. Because of course not. "And, uh, I think I have a crush on someone."

She winced after she said that, sounding so childish. If there was anything her brothers would snap awake for, it was that confession.

But, as usual, they just laid there.

"It's silly because he's kinda someone that I hated—well, no. Hated is the wrong word. *Resented*, I guess. I resented him because he had everything that I wanted and none of it seemed fair."

That was the crux of the matter, wasn't it? She told herself that she was better than all the people who bullied her. Smarter. Kinder. More patient. That her suffering had given her a better sense of character.

But really, she was mostly just jealous. She could only dream of the kind of things and experiences Benji had, and that made her feel weak, which in turn made her lump him in with all of the others.

Huh, she really wasn't as objective as she thought, was she?

"Guys, I wish you were here. Like, really here. I have so much to tell you."

Then again, what was stopping her? Leaning back, she started from the beginning and went from there.

When she eventually finished some moments later, she felt a bit better, like her brain had to hear everything out loud to process it all.

But still, as the silence crept in with only the sound of her brothers' machines and their steady breathing, she couldn't help but feel...

Alone.

She always felt so alone.

16

———

Benji

Benji found himself pacing in circles around his room, barefoot and in his pajama pants even though it was well past sun up.

As soon as he realized Dani had snuck out of the diner, he'd called her parents to make sure that she was all right. He had no idea where she was and was worried that something had happened to her.

But also, he didn't want to tell her parents outright that he had kind of lost her, so he very carefully beat around the bush to ask if she had gotten inside all right.

They'd answered that she had. After a bit of a pause, they asked if something had reminded her of her brothers while they were out. He'd kind of fumbled around with that answer before they informed him that she'd headed to the hospital to visit her siblings.

He had wished them goodnight and then that was that. He'd headed home and spent the entire night staring up at his ceiling, trying to figure out what to do.

No answers had come to him then, so the next morning he resolved to just go up to her and talk it out like adults. Because that's what they were, after all. She wasn't some puzzle to figure out. She was a human being.

Except the next day, she stayed locked in her house, not coming out the entire day. Benji waited all the way until it was well past the time to go, and when he didn't see so much as a glimpse of her, he had swallowed his pride and gone up to the door.

It was Mrs. Touhey who had answered, and when he had asked after her daughter, she told him that Dani wasn't feeling well and was taking the day off.

And the next day.

After that, he had resolved to stop asking because he felt like he was being creepily persistent.

It was just... he understood *why* she was embarrassed. He just didn't want her to feel that way. He wanted to tell her that he only blamed Rachel and finally understood so much of what she said.

But he couldn't do that if she never left the haven of her house.

So that was how he ended up in his apartment, walking in circles around his living room, wondering how he could talk to her. It wasn't even a matter of getting him a date again. He just wanted to comfort her. To tell her that he didn't think any less of her.

She had spent so many years being bullied in that passive-aggressive way—and apparently outright aggressive—with no one to stand up for her except her brothers. He wanted her to know that she wasn't totally alone.

He understood her.

Not completely, but enough to want to get to know her even better, if she'd let him.

"Come on, Benji," he groused to himself, something he only did when he was feeling *really* stuck. "*Think.*"

He started pacing again.

He'd texted his brothers late the previous night that he needed the morning off from chores. It was Sunday anyway, which was the day of the week they only cared for the animals and didn't do any serious work.

Wait... it was Sunday.

An idea came to him. It was Sunday, which definitely meant church. And when there was church, there was Keiko, and who better to talk to about Dani than the woman who he was pretty sure was her best friend?

Finally. That would be the way in. Either Keiko would help him or tell him that he needed to drop it and that would be that. And even if she told him neither, he was sure that she would be able to comfort Dani in the way only a best friend could.

Perfect.

Benji allowed himself an enthusiastic clap of his hands then strode toward his dresser, picking out Sunday clothes his Ma would approve of. With a pep in his step that he hadn't had since the date, he headed to the main house.

Of course, it was his Ma who he saw first, standing in the middle of the foyer and smoothing her dress as she waited for Ben to finish in the kitchen—judging by the sound of the fumbling from the room.

She wasn't alone, however. Another slender, older woman was standing across from her.

"Benji!" Ma said, face lighting up. "I don't often see you this early on a Sunday. You remember Chastity's mother, Mrs. Parker."

He walked over to his Ma and placed a small kiss on the top of her head before offering his hand to the other woman. "Pleased to see you again, Mrs. Parker. I remember you from when we were younger, but even if I didn't, Chastity talks an awful lot about you. She might be the only person I've met who loves their Ma as much as we do."

The woman laughed, a faraway look in her eyes. "Is that so? What a compliment then, coming from a Miller son. And which one are you?"

"I'm Benjamin. But most people call me Benji."

"Funny," the woman remarked. "I would have thought that Ben was named Benjamin."

Benji opened his mouth to tell her that she'd always known his name was Benjamin, but Ma subtly shook her head and he let it drop. If he remembered right, Mrs. Parker was still going through a lot of treatment for her sickness from the previous year.

"Anyway, Benji dear, to what do I owe the pleasure of seeing you today? Just a surprise blessing?"

He felt a bit sheepish at that. He didn't want to tell his mother that the only reason he had gotten himself out of bed in time to go to church was for a woman, so he quickly made up a reason that let him sound less shallow.

"Oh, you know, just thought with all the arson and doom and gloom going on that maybe I should go and thank God for all he's given us."

Huh, was it an extra sin to lie on the Lord's day? He resolved to be more careful with that.

"Oh, well I do quite like the sound of that. Never take for granted what we have, lest the Lord see fit to take it away."

"Amen."

"There! I have all the mini-quiches!" Chastity said, rushing out of the kitchen.

She was dressed smartly in a suit jacket and pencil skirt with Ben coming up behind her wearing a matching colored outfit.

"You've got to be kidding me," Benji said, looking over the two of them. "You two are dressing alike now?"

"They were a gift," Chastity said, a wan smile on her face that hinted that she didn't entirely mind her beau all suited up to match her. "We're just going to take a few pictures in them and then never do this again."

"Uh-huh," Benji agreed with his own grin.

"Wait, are you coming to church with us too?" That was Ben, who looked from Ma, to Mrs. Parker to Benji and he could almost see the steam coming out of his brother's ears as he tried to logistic it all out.

But it was the Lord's day, so Benji could cut him a little slack. "I was hoping to, but it seems like your truck is gonna be full. How about I just follow you guys?"

Besides, that would give him some wiggle room if he needed to divert his plans. He didn't know *why* he would need to do that, but he liked having the option available.

"Well, let's get going then," Ma said with a smile. "We need to get these to Keiko so she can put them in the fridge and write up allergy cards for them. You brought the recipes, right Chastity?"

She nodded, her dark hair bouncing, patting one of the sides of her suit. "It's in the pocket in here. I made sure it was legible too."

"Oh good. I can't tell you how much fun I had baking with you two this morning. We really must do it again," Ma said, looking from Chastity to Mrs. Parker.

"Definitely," Mrs. Parker agreed. "It felt so fulfilling to use those recipes that I just haven't had the energy for in years."

There was more friendly, grateful talk as the group migrated out to Ben's truck, but Benji slipped away to get into his own car. He normally liked that kind of stuff, but at the moment it was just reminding him of how he wished it could be with Dani.

Whoa.

That was a revelation.

Did he want something like Ben had?

Sure, he wouldn't lie that he'd been attracted to Dani, with her sharp gaze and sharper tongue and thick thighs. But being attracted to someone, wanting to spend a date or two with them, was *very* different than wanting what his brother had.

What his brother had was a *relationship.* Maybe even a soul mate. They were together all the time and were working together to build a future. It wasn't easy, given Chastity's ambitions and Ben's responsibilities, but he watched them work and work at it.

He'd always thought that all of that was far too exhausting, but as he watched the four of them pile into Ben's extended cab truck, he couldn't help but wonder if… maybe… that had changed for him.

Shouldn't he know before going and pestering a woman who clearly had some stuff to work through on her own? Was he putting his needs before hers?

He sat there, thinking for several moments. He needed to treat Dani like a human being. Not an objective or barn to fix. He wasn't going to be one of those men who chased a woman like she was some prize to be won and then placed on the mantle.

Ben began to pull the truck out of the drive, and Benji was snapped from his introspection. When had his life gotten so complicated? His biggest issue used to be juggling his brothers' issues, but suddenly he seemed to have plenty on his own.

Oh well. He would talk to Keiko and then try to sit down and figure out exactly what he wanted.

What was the worst that could happen?

Benji wasn't the greatest fan of sermons. Often, he felt pastors spent far too much time blustering and bloviating rather than just getting down and talking about the word. Ma said it was because he was too practical for his own good sometimes, but Benji guessed it was that when he studied the Bible, that was just what he wanted to do: study the Bible. No long songs, no other people clapping. Just him and the good book, figuring things out as he read and reread parts.

He found out he liked sermons even less when he was anxiously waiting to get to the breakfast mingling and find Keiko. Despite his family leaving plenty early, they still didn't arrive soon enough to catch her, since she was already reading stories to kids in the nursery. Thank fully, the mini-quiches were saved as an older lady had taken them and hauled them off to the fridge.

His leg bounced for several beats, jiggling the seat as the pastor lead the closing prayer. He didn't even realize he was doing it until Ma's hand gently rested on his knee.

"Sorry," he murmured.

"Nervous?" she whispered back, cracking open one of her eyes.

"No, just uh, got something to do."

"Something here at the church?"

It took a lot of willpower not to roll his eyes. That felt extra sacrilegious considering where they were.

"Ma, you're doing that thing."

"What thing?"

"The thing where you ask seemingly unassuming questions to whittle out some sort of secret."

"Oh, so you do have secrets then?"

"*Ma.*"

She giggled ever so lightly. "What, with what's happened with Ben and Bart, can you blame me for wondering if my most even-keeled son finally found someone who made his heart flutter?"

"Heart flutter? That sounds like a medical issue."

"You always did like to use humor to deflect. That's fine. I'm sure it has nothing to do with the Touhey's daughter."

Benji almost choked on his own spit, giving her a wide-eyed stare. Ma just smiled like the secret super-spy that she was and closed her eyes for the prayer.

Oh right.

That was still going on.

Somehow Benji managed to stop looking at his mother like she was completely right and get through the closing of the rest of the sermon without vibrating out of his seat. But as soon as it was done, he gave Ma a kiss on her cheek and bounded out into the main foyer where the bagels, donuts, and other breakfast items waited.

Sure enough, he saw Keiko standing by the coffee station, brewing another pot as she filled one of the dispensers. She was wearing a pretty, floaty dress in pale pink. It looked nice on her, and he felt a bit underdressed all of a sudden.

Maybe if he was going to talk to her about her best friend, he should have made himself more presentable.

Oh well. It was too late to change that now. Striding over to her, he gave her what he hoped was a charming grin.

"Hello there, Keiko."

She didn't startle at all, just calmly finished pouring then looked to him with a kind smile. "Benji, hello. I haven't seen you in a bit."

Did everyone know he liked to sleep in on Sundays? "Uh yeah, I've been busy."

"Helping the Touheys right?"

Right. She knew about that. "Yeah. It's been going pretty well. Another week or so and there won't be much more left for us to do."

"That's lovely to hear."

"Uh, yeah, it is."

Keiko's head tilted to the side, and she gave him a curious look. "You don't sound like you agree."

What was with the weirdly perceptive women all around him? Did he just have his emotions written across his face way more than he ever thought?

"Actually, I was hoping maybe I could talk to you."

"We're talking right now."

"Uh, in... private, maybe? Where no one could overhear?"

Keiko finally set all of the coffee stuff down and studied him for several beats. Benji couldn't help but feel like he was being scanned, assessed, and dissected in her keen gaze.

"All right. Let's go talk."

She walked away, her low heels clicking on the floor, and Benji quickly followed. She led him all the way down the hall, around the corner and to the kitchen. As soon as the door closed behind him, she turned to Benji with a grin.

"This is about Dani, isn't it?"

"What, is it tattooed on my forehead or something?"

"No, but I heard about a little snafu at the diner and I might have put two and two together."

Benji grimaced at that. Of course, word about that had gotten around. No wonder Dani was hiding in her house.

"Ah, that's unfortunate."

"Yeah. I never thought that Rachel would stoop to those levels. She was always vicious in high school, but it never got physical. I always thought that was something to be grateful for, but it looks like it was only because Dani didn't have anything Rachel wanted."

"I had no idea it was going to be like that. Otherwise, I never would have taken her to a place in town."

Keiko seemed to think for several moments before she spoke again. "I love this town. I love this church. I have found so much love in so many people."

Well, that was nice, but what did that—

"But I've also found so much pain, misery, and judgment. I've watched people hurt my friends and each other. Fought just for the right to exist.

"It wasn't easy moving here in middle school, the only Asian in all of our town and one of four people of color, including Chastity. Kids were cruel and adults could be ignorant, leaving me wondering if I was going to be alone."

"That all sounds pretty bad."

"Because it was. Very bad. But then I found Dani and her brothers in school. I found friends in theater and other clubs. I had people like Chastity to look up to. And then I found this church." Her smile was so sweet, so contented, that Benji could see how Dani found solace in her best friend. "It was like having a safe haven. And in that safe haven, I could find the good in this town. Everything worth cherishing."

"And Dani doesn't have a safe haven?"

"She did, with her family. But now that her brothers are in the hospital and she blames herself, all of that is gone. She's in a vulnerable position now, and a predator like Rachel could sense that."

"You think Rachel is a predator?"

"I think all people have the capacity to be predatory. She didn't like that Dani was trying to claim happiness that she didn't think she deserved and wanted to punish her. I think the only reason she took it so far was because she could tell Dani was already struggling with everything else."

"I can't believe you know all this, and you can just rattle it off like it's fact. And I was an idiot who thought I was going to change everyone's view of her single-handedly."

Keiko's gaze sharpened ever so slightly. "And why do you want to change people's view?"

"Because I think she's this great, impressive, brave person, and I don't understand why others don't see it."

"Others don't see it because they just see a fat young woman and they assign all the negative character traits they've been taught go hand in hand with someone being plus-sized. They don't value her strength because her muscles aren't visible. They want her to be pretty how they expect her to be pretty, and nothing else will ever be enough."

"But I don't get it," Benji said, the conversation going a direction he hadn't expected. "Missy is pretty the way people expect her to be pretty, but she used to get hassled all the time."

Keiko laughed ever so lightly at that, but the sound was dry and knowing. "I think you've found one of the catch-twenty-twos of being an outsider and a woman in this town. There's no winning."

"How did I never see this before?"

Benji sat on one of the stools. More and more of Dani was making sense, but at the same time, he was feeling pretty stupid for not catching on earlier.

"Because people have never and will never treat your family that way. You've been shielded from all the negative things that Dani's been enduring her whole life. So, if you came here to ask why she doesn't trust you, that would be why."

"Actually," Benji said with a sigh, rubbing his temples. "I was hoping to come to you to ask you how to fix all of this."

"Fix what?"

"How I messed up. She snuck out of the restaurant and went home, and now she's been hiding for days. I get that she might be embarrassed, or hurt, or any number of those things, but I want her to feel better and know she's not alone."

"Why?"

Benji looked to her in surprise, his gaze having been drawn to the floor as he imagined Dani laying in her bed, crying and lonesome.

"Why what?"

"Why do you want to fix it? Is it some need to save the day? You want her to date you? You have some compulsion to be a hero, or do you just like a good project?"

"No, none of those things! I mean—" He paused to think. It would do no good to get flustered and say something wrong. "Yes, I'm attracted to Dani. And yes, I would like it if she'd let me get a do-over on the date, but that's not *why* I want her to feel better.

"I want to support her, to help her get over this because she deserves it. For some reason, she seems to have been given this awful hand that never relents, and I wish she could get a break! You know?

"She works hard, she tries to do right by her family. She doesn't bother anybody. So, if I can help her, if I can make all of these bad things go away for a little while, then that seems more than worth it to me."

A soft hand on his shoulder had him looking up at Keiko's face. "You know, I always wondered if you Miller boys would use your influence to change this town for the better, and so far I haven't been disappointed."

"What do you mean? My brothers and I haven't changed anything."

He racked his brain to try to think of anything exceptionally special that they had done, but he came up empty. Sure, he had been helping the Touheys, but that wasn't town-changing.

She seemed to consider that. "Perhaps it's best that you don't see it. But anyway, yes, I will help you."

"Wait, really?"

She nodded emphatically. "What can I say? It's not often that a young, charming man comes to me, begging for help to treat my best friend like she deserves. I'm happy to help you make Dani feel better. And if something happens between the two of you because of that..." She shrugged. "Then perhaps it was meant to be."

Benji was on his feet and pulling her into a hug before his brain even processed what she was saying. It was a quick act, but when he let her go, she caught his chin with her tiny, slender fingers.

"But I should make one thing clear. I love Dani so much that my heart often aches. If you do anything to hurt her, I will do a very unchristian thing and make your life utterly miserable."

Benji absolutely believed her. "I'll make sure to remember that."

"Good." She let go of his face and crossed to the fridge to pull out a pitcher of tea and a carton of juice. "That would do you well. Come, help with this and we'll get started on our plan."

"And what's our jumping off point?"

"Well, first I'm going to have you tell me about your date, every exact detail, and we'll go from there."

"That makes sense to me."

17

———

Danielle

*D*ani flopped back across her bed, looking up at the ceiling and rethinking all of the depressing, terrible things that she had been thinking over the past few days.

Her parents thought that she had a stomach virus that wasn't letting up, but in reality, it was more of a personal thing that was affecting her far more than it had any right to.

One bad date wasn't going to kill her. She'd been through worse and survived. So why was she moping around like it was the end of the world? She kept telling herself to get up and move on with her life, but she would just always end up in the same place again, laying across her bed and cycling through all those self-destructive thoughts.

Being humiliated by Rachel had made her feel small and weak. She wasn't small and weak, she knew that. Anyone could get hot food dumped on their head, and it spoke nothing of their character. But as much as she told herself that, all she really succeeded in doing was reminding herself of how other people in town loathed her and that she was powerless to do a single thing about it.

She was sure the story had already gone through town like a wildfire, Rachel and her cronies finding a way to twist it to make Dani the villain. That thought made her sense of right and wrong flare up, which would always end in nausea because there just wasn't anything she could *do.*

And, of course, there was the embarrassment of all of it happening in front of Benji. He had seen how much of an outcast she was, and how all her strength was really just a farce. Yet again she was struck by her silliness at hoping that something could happen between them, even if it was all the way in the back of her mind.

A soft knock sounded on her door and Dani had to withhold a groan. That wasn't a nice sound to make when it was probably just her mother checking on her for the fourth time that day. Two of Mom's sons were in the hospital. It wasn't like Dani could blame her for being a bit hypercautious when she thought her third child was ill too.

"Hey, Dani?"

Wait, that definitely wasn't her mother's voice.

Dani sat up to see Keiko at the door, dressed in a loose T-shirt and jeans. She always looked great no matter how she was dressed, and Dani was reminded that she hadn't changed her own clothes in two days. She probably looked like a troll.

"Keiko, what are you doing here?"

"I was hoping to talk actually."

Dani looked over her friend and then flopped back with a groan. "You know about the diner?"

"I know about the diner," she said with a nod, coming to join Dani over on the bed. "You know, your parents almost didn't let me up here. Apparently, you've been sick with a stomach bug for a few days?"

"Yeah. A real virulent one, so you should probably go before you catch something."

Keiko reached over and ruffled Dani's semi-greasy hair. "Uh-huh, just like the bad stomach bug you got in freshmen year when you acci-dentally bled through your pants in school?"

Dani groaned. "Why did you have to remind me of that?"

"Because I want you to remember that things have been worse. The teasing and whispers that went on for months and you survived. And back then you had to see those people every single day."

"Ugh, is this where you tell me that I should ignore all those people and words can't hurt me? Because I don't know how much you know, but that gravy was *hot*."

"No, I'm not stupid enough to tell you that people's words or opin-ions don't matter. I spend multiple days a week just going over the words of a very old book and living my life by them. I know all of this hurts, and I would never invalidate how you feel by telling you that you shouldn't let them get to you."

"Huh, thanks then, Keiko." Dani straightened and tried to make herself look less like a homeless person. "But you don't have enough cookies or quesadillas on you for this to be a commiseration trip, so why *are* you here?"

Keiko smiled dreamily, looking to the ceiling. "I *do* love quesadillas. But no, this isn't a commiseration visit. Although I'm not telling you that you shouldn't care about what people say, I'm here to remind you that things are a lot different now. It's not high school, with you and me against the world once your brothers graduated."

"Then why do I feel like I'm right back there?"

"Because you've built up all your defenses to survive in that envi-ronment. I know it's hard, but don't you think there are a couple of them that you could drop and still live a fulfilling life?"

Dani snorted. "Like what?"

"Like automatically assuming the worst in people to preemptively defend yourself."

Ouch. She may have had a point, but that didn't mean that Dani liked it. "But you have to admit, most people are pretty terrible and worth defending yourself from."

"I would argue against 'most,' but I won't deny that there are some really vicious losers out there. But not *everyone*. Don't you ever wonder if, perhaps, you've missed out on someone who could be a really great addition to your life because you're so quick to believe that everyone is out to hurt you?"

Her mind instantly went to Benji. There was the tiniest sliver of hope in her that maybe he didn't judge her for the incident in the diner. That he wasn't mad that she had run away, or thought she was absolutely childish because of the way she had reacted.

Because how could he not take it personally? She had basically ghosted him on their first date instead of talking to him like an adult, then ran all the way to the city to make sure he couldn't see her. Then she proceeded to skulk in her room for a few days like a hormonal teenager. How on earth would he ever want to talk to her again after that kind of behavior?

But the thought of facing him, of being rejected, hurt more than it had any right to, and she flopped right back onto her bed again.

"I dunno, maybe," she answered, only barely remembering that Keiko had asked her a question. Unless it had been rhetorical, but sometimes it was hard to tell with her calm friend.

"Hmm, maybe indeed." She was quiet for several long moments before she too flopped on the bed, reaching over to entwine her finger with Dani's. Her hands were so soft, missing all of the callouses and scars that Dani's had from ranch life.

The touch was comforting, helping fill some of the ache and embarrassment that had been ravaging her mood for the past few days.

"Can I ask you a question?" Keiko asked finally, her voice soft and soothing enough not to break the calming mood that had settled over the room.

"You know you can."

"You sure? It's a bit personal."

"You're my best friend. Personal questions and secrets are supposed to be like half of our conversations."

"Really? I didn't know that it had been quantified. Do you have any studies to back that up?"

Dani shook their joined hands. "Come on, out with it. I can tell when you're beating around the bush."

"Well, since we're talking about the diner, why were you there with Benji Miller?"

Oh.

Of course, she would ask that.

That was the most titillating part of the gossip, right? What was *he* doing with someone like *her*?

She knew that Keiko didn't think about it in that negative light, but she couldn't stop that dour, mouthy part of her brain from reiterating it anyway.

"We were having a meal."

"But *why*? Was he doing a favor to your parents? Were you doing him a favor? Were you..." She hesitated a moment, as if she wasn't sure she should say what she was thinking. "...on a date?"

"Why does it matter?"

Keiko rolled over so that she was staring at Dani's profile. "Because I want to know what you think of him. Honestly."

"*Why?*"

"Because I want to know what's on my best friend's mind. Do you think he set you up? Were you just going out to dinner with him as a thank-you? I know that a lot has been going on in your life lately, and I feel like we haven't talked much about it all."

A tendril of guilt took hold of Dani. It *had* been a while since she and Keiko had gabbed. Maybe since the grocery store almost a month ago. That *was* far too long, but there'd just been so much going on in her head! "*Yes.* I was on a date."

She could feel Keiko perk up beside her and it was enough to make the corner of her mouth turn up in a grin.

"Who asked who?" Keiko asked.

"Does that matter?"

"*Yes.* Tell me everything. Come on."

"I feel like this is unfair. You've never spilled any deep boy secrets to me."

"That's because I've never had any deep boy secrets. I've never even had a crush that wasn't buried in the pages of a book. Now come on, let me live a little vicariously, okay?"

"Fine. I asked him."

"Why?"

"What, is that the question of the day?"

"*Dani.*"

It was so easy to slip back into their usual banter, even though they were talking about something they'd never had to discuss before. It settled even more of Dani's mood, and she was able to articulate what had been churning in a never-ending cyclone in her mind.

"I asked him because he was turning all of my rules upside down. He was nice, but he didn't seem to want anything. And he was funny. And the way he *looked* at me, I..." she threw her arm over her face and groaned. "It was like I was finally being *seen.*"

"And I suppose it doesn't hurt that he's drop-dead gorgeous."

Dani rolled onto her own side, facing her friend. "I mean, it didn't *hurt*, but that wasn't a deciding factor. There are plenty of attractive guys in town, and I'm not attracted to them."

"Yeah, there are some good-looking guys, but any *that* attractive? I dunno."

"Okay, yes. Benji is very good-looking. He's got those eyes, and that jaw, and that *hair.*" She shook her head, stopping herself from getting too caught up in it. "But that's beside the point. I asked him out because I wanted to see if he really was different."

"And you wanted to see if he was different because you were attracted to him?"

"Yeah, I guess."

"Dani, do you want to date Benji Miller?"

Boy, she just went right for the throat, didn't she? Dani didn't answer right away, fearing what might happen if she admitted it out loud. She couldn't believe that she was twenty-six and panting over the hot jock like all those girls she used to look down on in high school. She had thought she was so much better them then, but really... they weren't that different.

Except for the whole bullying thing. That was a pretty stark contrast.

"Yes," she said finally, her heart squeezing so tightly in her chest that it made her feel flush all over. "I would like to date Benji Miller." More words rushed out of her immediately, wanting to cover up the chink in her armor that she had just let show. "But I know how stupid that is. Like really. There's no way someone *that* rich and handsome isn't secretly evil, and also, people like him don't date people like me."

Keiko's gaze grew serious. "What do you mean by that?"

"Aw, come on, you know what I mean."

"No. I don't. You're a stubborn, intense person, yes. You're determined and fierce, and you don't trust very easily, but none of those make you undatable, so I want to know what you mean."

"Come on. I'm the fat girl, and he's... well, he's what he is. I'm poor, and his family is mega rich. They don't even know what it's like to worry about money. He's charming and makes everybody feel good, and I usually can't stop myself from correcting someone if they say something I think is wrong."

"Dani, don't you normally love your body? Ever since we were young, I remember you telling me that fat is just an adjective, not a bad word. Where is this self-consciousness streak coming from?"

"Yeah, I know that normally, but when I look at Benji, sometimes I can only think about all the things that I'm sure he believes. I assume that he's like everyone else in high school, and even now."

"Hmm, I think there's a phrase about what assuming does."

"Ugh, I know. How did I get to be such a mess? I always thought I had it all together."

"Well, you did suffer a pretty big trauma, and two of your closest loved ones are currently in the hospital, which you blame yourself for. I've always suspected you've struggled with depression your whole life, but I think recent events might have really aggravated it."

"Thanks for the psychoanalysis," Dani groused, turning over her friend's words in her head.

They made a sort of sense, but they also made Dani feel worse. Depression? Trauma? Those were things she was just supposed to power through.

"No problem. I live to serve. Now, long term, I think perhaps seeing a counselor or therapist wouldn't hurt. But in the meantime, I think I know what might help."

"Oh, what's that?" Dani asked.

Suddenly she was exhausted. So exhausted, and she just wanted to sink into her mattress and never come out.

"Here, come with me. We're going to get you showered and cleaned up."

"Aw, come on, Keiko. I really don't wanna go outside."

"I know, which is why we're doing exactly that. Up and at 'em. You'll feel better if you clean all that guilt and oil off yourself."

Dani chuckled a bit to herself. "Yes, that's me. Guilt and oil."

"Yeah, yeah. Come on now."

Keiko got up, pulling Dani with her, who let the slighter woman rouse her to her feet. In that steely but quiet way of hers, Keiko herded her toward the bathroom and started to run the water. But when she tried to peel off Dani's shirt, that was when she finally spoke up.

"I can handle this part myself."

"You sure? I couldn't tell considering that this shirt seems like it's been on your body far longer than it was supposed to be."

"Hardy har. You're hilarious. I'll shower, all right? Clean behind my ears and everything. I promise."

"All right. I'll go get you a glass of water and a change of clothes. I'm thinking that you and I should take a day together. Reconnect, blow off some steam, you know the drill."

Dani smiled to herself. She really was lucky to have someone like Keiko in her life. She didn't think that she would have survived high school without her friendship.

And it turned out she was pretty right. While the shower didn't exactly cure all her ills and make her feel any less embarrassed about pulling the Great Escape on Benji, it did help her feel slightly less miserable.

Almost refreshed.

A knock sounded at the door when she was in the middle of giving herself a really good scrub. She barely heard it over the shower water and turned the spray down.

"Uh, hello?"

"It's Keiko. I wanted to put the water and change of clothes on the sink. Can I come in?"

Living in a small, two-story house with five people and only one bathroom, the Touheys had long since learned to get *very* opaque shower curtains in case someone needed to use the restroom while someone else was showering. Dani made sure she was relatively shielded enough before answering.

"Sure, come on in."

It wasn't that Dani was ashamed of her body most of the time, and it wasn't that she distrusted Keiko, but she had always been private with her body, no matter who she was with. It was *hers*, really the only thing that she had any inherent ownership of, and so she was incredibly selective of who she shared it with.

And by selective, she meant absolutely no one.

"I'll be down in the kitchen when you're done. No hurry. I want you to take as much time as you need."

"Don't worry," Dani said with a laugh, feeling like she was almost returning to her old self. "I don't know how I'd forgotten how nice a steaming hot shower is in just a couple of days."

"Well, being stuck in your own misery loop can do that to people."

"Fair point."

True to her word, Keiko set the things on the sink and headed right back out. Dani enjoyed somewhere between five to ten minutes more of the shower before kicking herself out. She didn't want to use up all the hot water in case her parents wanted to take a turn in the next few hours. Granted, they were usually early risers, but it never hurt to be considerate.

Once she was out, she thoroughly dried herself, actually taking the time to blow dry her hair on cool and brush it out. There were still a couple of knots left over even after her thorough conditioning, and that took a bit of work with her paddle brush to get out.

When she was finally all done and dressed, she looked in the mirror. There, that was more like the Dani she knew. Less bridge troll and more curvy woman who knew how to take care of herself.

Yeah.

Now she just had to not think about Benji for the rest of the day.

She had a feeling that was easier said than done.

18

Danielle

*D*ani headed down the stairs, empty glass in hand. She found Keiko in the kitchen, standing in front of the window and conversing softly with Dani's parents.

"I'm ready," she said, giving her parents a smile.

They looked relieved, and she felt a bit guilty again at worrying them. She really had been selfish the past couple of days, hadn't she? It was a wonder she had never joined the theater club with Keiko considering how dramatically she had let herself wither.

Oh well. What was done was done. She was moving forward, as Keiko said.

"Great," Keiko said, pushing off of the counter and reaching her hand out again. "Let's go."

"Where are we headed? We could go to the city to hit up the theater..."

Dani couldn't remember the last time that she had been to a movie.

Tickets were so expensive, and she was always so busy, but today seemed like a day to take care of herself.

"You'll see."

"What do you mean, you'll see?"

But Keiko didn't answer. She just grabbed Dani's hand and hurried her out the door, her smile broad and far too sneaky.

Before Dani could object, or even really figure out what was happening, she was out on the small porch, down the steps and walking through the garden.

She wasn't quite sure what she was expecting, but it certainly wasn't Benji, standing there in a nice shirt, tie and jeans, looking at her like she was the sun that had just risen.

All of the air *whooshed* out of her and she looked to Keiko in confusion. "What is going on?"

"Remember what I said about maybe not assuming the worst in people? If you're willing to take a chance, I think you could have a really fun day today."

Dani looked at her friend incredulously. "You set me up!"

Her eyes crinkled when she smiled in the way that only Keiko could. "I'm giving you a choice. If you want to walk away and go right up to your room, you can. But I think, maybe, that you really don't want to do that."

Dani looked from her friend to Benji and back. He looked so handsome, all clean-cut and dressed up, staring at her with that look that made her want to believe all sorts of impossible things.

"I, uh... I suppose I could give it a try."

"Good," she said, letting go of Dani's hand. "That's all I ask."

Then she was walking off toward the house, leaving the two together.

"Uh, so... what are you doing here?" Dani started with, wincing at the silly question. But Benji just took it in stride, walking right up to her and extending his hand.

"Hopefully showing you that I just might be worth trusting."

"But why would you care after I—"

He shook his head. "Let's not talk about that awful woman and that awful ending. We all respond to stress differently, and you did what you thought what you needed to do given the situation."

She gently placed her hand in his, and he led her to the end of the garden where a small tent was set up, chiffon curtains hanging in gauzy layers around the edges.

"But what I'd like to do, is maybe give you some pleasant memories to wipe away all of that awfulness."

"That's not really how memories work," she murmured, looking at the table set in the center of the mini-tent with a chair on either side of it. "But okay."

He led her all the way up to one of the chairs and pulled it back, looking at her expectantly. She sat down, and he pushed her chair up to the table.

Now that she was closer, she could see that there was a pitcher of some sort of sparkling drink and little tea snacks or whatever they were called. They were cute, pretty and looked utterly delicious.

"What's all this?" she asked, looking over the table curiously.

"The best way to start the day is a healthy breakfast, and if you're game, I'd like to think I have a good day planned for us."

"Breakfast? It's past eleven."

Why did she have to question everything? She bit her lip, looking at him with an apologetic expression, but he just smiled and handed her a plate.

"Help yourself," he said, picking up what looked like a tiny cucumber sandwich and popping it in his mouth. "And this is sparkling lemonade if you're thirsty."

Dani's eyebrows went up to her hairline. "I didn't even know that was a thing."

"Well, I'm sure that it doesn't compare to your homemade mixture, but my Ma swears by this stuff."

"Is your Ma the one who put you up to this?" she asked cautiously.

"No. Hardly. Like I'd ever let her know how badly I botched our first date."

"You?" she asked incredulously. "Rachel was the one who ruined everything, and then I made it worse by climbing out the window like some sort of reverse-burglar."

"Reverse burglar? Hah, I like that." He smiled at her, and his eyes did that thing again that made her heart race. "But I don't think I'd complain about you creeping through my window."

She blushed and looked down at her plate. "I don't understand. I was really immature. You should be furious with me."

"You think so?" He rested that chin of his in his hand, his normal shadow of stubble gone.

Huh, he had completely clean-shaven his face just for her. Or was she looking too far into that?

"The way I see it, I should have known better. It's because I didn't take your warnings about people seriously that we ended up somewhere you got hurt."

"I wasn't hurt!" she objected automatically before he gave her a patient look. "I mean... not really hurt. Not like—"

"Your brothers?" he asked. "Dani, I know you've got a lot of conflicting emotions there, and we're not to the place yet where you'd share those with me, but you gotta stop comparing everything in life to that level of tragedy. You're allowed to be upset that an old bully got your goat. You're allowed to be embarrassed that you were carried through a restaurant. Your pain is real. You don't have to end up in the hospital in an induced coma to justify how you feel."

She leaned forward, resting her head in her hands so she could escape that intense look of his. "I don't understand why you're doing all of this for me. I've been nothing but mean to you. This past month I've been on some of the worst behavior of my life."

"Dani, you've had an arsonist attack your home, the place you feel safe, the place where the people you love live, *twice*. I can't imagine the sort of anxiety and stress that would bring on. But I've seen you try to shoulder it all, and I want you to know, you don't have to. Okay?"

She could feel tears pricking at the corners of her eyes and all she wanted to do was get off the rollercoaster of emotions that someone had strapped her into.

"I... it's just a lot, okay? I want to believe you. That you're good and you want to help me, but it's so hard to not listen to that nasty voice inside of me that tells me you're just like everyone else."

"I know," he said, his hand slowly sliding across the table. It was a peace offering, it seemed, and she took several deep breaths before letting her own palm rest on top of his. "And I'm not asking you to just hand me the keys to your life and treat me like Keiko."

"What are you asking for, then?" she asked, eager to keep him talking. Because if he was talking, then she didn't have to.

"For you to give me today. That's it. Nothing more, and nothing less."

She took another deep breath, gathering herself. "I can do that."

"Good," he flashed her a smile that made her heart flutter even more, and she almost had to pinch herself to make sure she wasn't dreaming. "You should try all these snacks though. I got them from this specialty place in the city, and they're really good."

"You went all the way to the city for these?"

He shook his head. "Nah, I was busy fixing my face this morning and working on, uh, a couple other things. I ordered them online yesterday and had them delivered this morning."

"I can't believe you went through all of this for me," Dani said, shaking her head.

"Well, you're worth it."

Another blush and she reached over to the closest treat, shoving it into her mouth. It turned out to be some sort of citrusy macaroon and her eyes closed in ecstasy.

"Oh wow, that's good," she practically moaned, holding her hand in front of her mouth in an effort to be at least a little polite.

"Glad you like it. And don't worry about any leftovers. Keiko said she'd decimate them after we move on. Although I don't know how much damage she can do."

Dani swallowed the delicious food and allowed herself a snort. "You have no idea. Keiko can put it away better than anybody I know."

"Really? But she's so... so..."

"Itty bitty? Yeah, it's pretty astounding when you see it. Maybe we should all take a trip to the city sometime and go to this all-you-can-eat Mexican buffet that she's crazy about."

"Oh, so does that mean you'll want to hang out with me again?" he countered, giving her a snarky look.

"Maybe, I don't know. I suppose that depends on how today goes, since you've apparently got all these plans."

"I do indeed."

They fell into a comfortable sort of quiet as they munched on the snacks. It wasn't super filling fare, but it was all very tasty. It didn't weigh her down or get the too full feeling like mac n' cheese or a meaty meal would.

After the pitcher was drained and maybe a half an hour or so passed, Dani felt like she was ready to move on. Her curiosity was building up anticipation in her, urging her onward.

"Are you ready to head out?" she asked, looking at Benji.

"If you are," he said, putting some sort of smoked salmon thing onto a crouton-like piece of bread that she could tell was expensive, then popping it into his mouth.

"Yeah, I think I'm to the point where I want to know what you're up to."

"What I'm up to? You make me sound so sneaky."

"Well, you did just enlist my best friend to trick me out of the house and onto this... adventure."

"Ow, *trick*? Such hard language." He stood and offered her his hand. "Dani, are you ready for a full day of being wooed and generally treated like the lovely lady that you are?"

"Lady?" she asked dubiously. "I think I wear far too many overalls for that."

"You and I both know that denim and other clothes have no bearing on if you're a woman or not."

"Well, maybe..." She took his hand as he gently pulled her up. Together, they walked back in the direction of the house before turning a bit to the side. "What? Is the second destination my vegetable garden?"

"Not quite, but it is waiting for you beside your vegetable garden."

"Huh. It's *waiting* for me?"

"Uh-huh."

"Interesting."

"You're not going to figure it out."

She could hear the smirk in his voice. "Is that so?"

"Yeah, that's so."

Her mind bounced about a dozen things it could be, but none of them made sense. She was so deep in her own thought that they ended up around the shed and in front of the garden without even realizing it.

"Is that... Is that a *buggy*?" she asked, eyes going wide.

That couldn't be. That was absolutely impossible. And yet what was standing in front of her could only be the small carriage that used to be so popular on the frontier.

There was a different horse standing there than the one he normally rode around on, thicker and taller with full tack on. He was attached to a beautiful, two-wheeled setup, the wood all polished to such a bright shine that the glint was almost blinding.

The sun canopy overhead was a light blue, much brighter and cheerier than the solid black she was used to seeing in history books, and the cushioned bench was a more royal version of the shade.

Even the spokes of the wheels had been painted a bright and happy gold, making the entire thing look refined and expensive without being gaudy.

"How did you even get this?" she asked, rushing to it but making sure she was far enough not to spook the horse with her sudden movement. "This is *amazing*."

"Glad you like it." He moseyed up beside her and offered his hand again, but she wasn't ready to get in quite yet.

"No, seriously, how did you get your hands on this?"

"Hah, well, to be honest, this was originally a gift I was working on in my spare time so that Pa and Ben could take their ladies on romantic rides. But then Bart and Missy started to be a thing so I figured they could use it too."

"But I'm not any of those people."

"No. You're not. But we all agreed that you should be the first one to test it out."

"Really?" Dani didn't know what to say. The buggy in front of her was *beautiful* and she couldn't believe that Benji had built it himself. "I can't believe you made this."

"Well, I can't take all the credit. I was the one who started it and worked on it at first last year, but my brothers have been chipping in. Especially Bart, considering how much better he's been lately. Makes a real good wrench monkey."

Dani reached out tentatively, her fingers gliding along the smooth, polished wood. "This is... this is really amazing, you know that."

He didn't answer for a moment, so she pried her gaze away from the work of art in front of her to see him looking at her, a flush over his face and his eyes much more intense than she was prepared for.

"It means a lot to hear you say that."

"Well, I mean it," she finished weakly before taking his hand and letting him help her up into the seat. Once she was settled, he slid in next to her and reached for the reins. "So where are we going?" she asked once she had her wits about her again.

She felt like one of those heroines in those old books about when the west was being settled, endless possibilities in front of her and not a care in the world for small-town politics. In those books looks didn't matter, or makeup or designer clothes, or any of that stuff. It was just people, learning and living and surviving together against the odds.

"There's a couple places I want to take you. Places I guarantee you've never seen."

"Oh really?" Dani asked, nudging him playfully. "I've lived here all my life. I'm pretty sure there isn't a part of this town I haven't seen before, and you're not gonna take me much father considering the pretty thing we're in."

"We'll see then." He gave her a wink, and she tried not to flush.

It felt like her entire body was next to a live wire, the hairs on the back of her neck standing on edge. Electric. *Alive*. Once more she found herself wanting to believe in things that the snappy, mean voice in her head told her could never happen.

After all, hadn't Keiko asked her to let her walls down at least a little?

Content to just be in the moment and not overthink it, she pressed a little closer into his side and looked out at their surroundings. The hottest part of the summer had passed, leaving their midday ride pleasantly warm with a nice breeze from over the plains. The canopy above them provided plenty of shade, so Dani didn't have to worry about any more freckles appearing on her fairly tanned skin.

The sky was so beautiful, stretching out all around them like a blue blanket, their canopy almost able to blend into it. She wondered briefly about painting clouds along the underside of it, but quickly decided that it was perfect the way it was.

The grass was a deep viridian, knee-high and only growing higher as it slowly transitioned into the long, wild strands of gold and yellow. Then, as they passed a short outcropping of rock and a gully that had once been an irrigation ditch, it all leveled out to the flat expanse of green that divided their property from the Miller's.

Ah, she should have guessed.

The Miller's large, sprawling acreage was indeed the only part of town that she had never been to. She'd often wondered how it looked, considering how wealthy they were, but had always resented them too much to ever check them out herself. It seemed that she was about to finally have her tour.

Sure enough, she saw a fence post in the distance and then Benji was gently pulling on the reins. The horse turned, smooth as butter, and they moved along the *very* lengthy barrier.

"Geez, do you guys really have a fence around all of your land? You know deforestation is a bad thing, right?"

He laughed at that, the sound making her feel warm in her chest. "No, we have it around the house and a few other areas to make sure the little ones don't get lost."

"Little ones?" As far as she knew, none of the Miller boys had popped out babies yet. Although the bet was on the eldest because the way he and his wife Chastity looked at each other always seemed to be like they were about to melt into each other.

"Yeah, our cousins, and our cousin's cousins and so on and so forth that live on the ranch. You know, I don't think most of them are actually related to us, but we've got some worker lines going back four generations, and if that's not family, I don't know what is."

"Wow, that's really hard for me to wrap my head around," Dani said honestly.

Her family's ranch was her full-time job, along with her brothers and parents. And if any of them ever had kids, it'd probably be their job too. They couldn't afford to bring on workers, but there was always so much work to do. It grated against Dani's nerves that there was always something left unfinished at the end of the day, so she couldn't imagine having it all... just... *done.*

By other people.

Other people who were paid *really* nice wages, according to the local gossip.

"It's all right. Your family will get there someday."

"You think so?" she asked, raising an eyebrow and giving him a look. But he seemed sincere.

"Yeah. And... Bradley is probably gonna kill me for mentioning it, but I've been eyeing your setup."

"Eyeing it? You've been helping us rebuild it for a month."

"Okay, you have a point. But what I mean is you guys have a real good thing going with your goats. One that we can't even touch. Apparently, my grandparents tried it once, and, for whatever reason, it didn't work out. Lost a *lot* of money."

"Wait, your brother doesn't want me to know that two generations ago a Miller managed to make a bad financial decision?"

Another chuckle sounded from Benji. "No, not that. I mean he wouldn't want me to tell you that I've been looking into maybe investing in your business. Diversifying my portfolio a bit."

Dani stared at him like he had grown a second head, because to her, it seemed like he had. "I'm sorry, what?"

"I'm not trying to buy you out or anything. Or bribe you, either. It's just that I've been learning all sorts of stuff from my little brother, and the most common lesson is that we can't rely on the same old same old if we want to stay on top of things. We should always be reaching out and expanding so we can adapt if certain things go belly up."

"And you think my family is a good investment?"

Dani felt like she was talking in slow motion, but she couldn't help it. Never in a million years had she ever thought a Miller would want to have anything to do with their ranch.

"Yeah. I mean, I know it's a bit sticky considering what's going on between us, but I do sincerely mean it. I got the idea back when I was helping you milk those goats and I saw your setup. You had soaps, milk, cheese, some salves. Your Ma practically forced me to take a whole basket of them the next day, and I gotta tell ya, the bars of soap were snatched out of that basket within two days and the food disappeared before that.

"And it was delicious. That cheese? Incredible. It tasted like stuff that would have to be special ordered from some really expensive gourmet shop."

Dani felt her temperature rise, pride coloring her cheeks. She liked it when people complimented the hard work of her and her family. They put a lot of their lives into making sure everything was successful, so it always was nice to be appreciated.

"Why didn't you ever say anything?"

"Well, because I wasn't sure. I asked Bradley to crunch some numbers and tell me if my idea was dumb or not. His initial findings were that it was worth looking into, so he's in that secondary phase now."

"Wow, that sounds so official."

"Everything sounds official with Bradley. He's a real wiz. Don't know where he gets it from because none of us have anything like it."

"I guess he's just a prodigy."

"Don't tell him that. Sometimes I worry that his head is gonna pop right off his shoulders from all the ego-stroking our parents do with him."

Dani peeked at him out of the corner of her eyes, eager to use humor to deflect a lot of the intense feelings that were flowing through her. "Do I detect the slightest bit of sibling rivalry?"

His cheeks colored a bit. "I dunno. Maybe. I guess I might have a little bit of that middle child syndrome."

"What, do you mean to tell me that the Millers aren't absolutely perfect?" she said in mock horror, pressing her hand to her chest.

"Yeah, yeah, yuk it up. We're human just like the rest of you peasants."

That startled a laugh out of her, a real, bellyful one that made her tilt her head back and just revel in the moment. It kept up for what was probably a ridiculous amount of time, not stopping until the buggy came to a halt.

"Huh?" she asked, wiping happy tears from her eyes.

It still took a couple more blinks before she could see properly, and she realized she was in the middle of a tree grove overlooking a beautiful pond.

"Oh wow," she said, mirth draining from her as she took in the beautiful site all around her.

There were ducks and geese all around, with even a few swans. They were far enough away that Dani could appreciate their aesthetic without worrying about the vicious little raptors getting any funny ideas in their birdie brains.

"This doesn't even look real," she said.

"I know, right? I have to be honest, but my brother told me about this place. Said it was a nice place to sit and watch the clouds go by."

He got out of the buggy, tying the horse off to a tree before coming back to help her out. Dani didn't need it, of course, but it was real nice to be pampered so. It didn't feel patronizing like it might have with other people. It just made her feel...

Appreciated.

Once her feet were on the ground, he went and grabbed a blanket to spread out in the center of the grove. Dani settled down, happy that she had taken a chance. She was still a bit mystified and overwhelmed, but she was going to settle in for a date that made her feel like anything could be possible.

Because when she looked at Benji, that possibility seemed more and more real.

19

Benji

If Benji could stare at Dani without blinking forever, he'd sign up in a heartbeat. He hadn't been expecting it but seeing her as she walked out of that house, dressed in a cute top and comfortable pants, washed up and smiling, had felt like lightning striking him right down his center.

He had been so afraid of what he might see. That her burns were worse than he thought, or her lips would curl in distaste at the very sight of him. But it wasn't like that at all. Sure, she looked shocked to see him—that was the whole plan. Yet there was something else there, under the surprise. Something... hopeful, perhaps?

And now that he sat next to her on the blanket he brought, telling her about the lake and the grove and how one particularly mean swan liked to terrorize all the children on the ranch, he couldn't help but feel that same hope again.

Her eyes caught his and his story faltered out, his brain far too distracted by the way the sun was reflecting in her pretty gaze.

"Why are you doing all this?" she asked again, her tone low. Like she was afraid if she spoke too loudly, he would disappear in a cloud of smoke.

But he wasn't going anywhere. It'd taken a lot of planning to get to this point, and he wasn't about to waste it all.

"Like I said, you deserve it."

Her lashes fluttered and she tipped her face up ever so slightly.

She had a unique look to her, round cheeks but a squared jaw, fine features that all blended into each other like a painting. She looked so angelic in the light, surrounded by the trees, that he couldn't help but lean towards her slightly.

"How can you say that so easily?"

"Because I mean it."

It was adorable watching her cheeks turn pink as her eyes flicked away. "People don't talk like that, you know. Not unless they're looking for something."

"I promise you, the only thing I'm looking for right in this moment is for you to have a good day."

"Really?" she asked, her lashes fluttering before their gazes joined again. "That's the *only* thing you want?"

He was about to agree when what she said caught up with him. Wait, was she *flirting* with him? That tone had a whole lot more weight behind it than the normal easy, breezy zingers she was so quick with.

"I, well, I mean..." He shook his head and decided to come out with it. "There are a whole lot of things I want, Dani. And I wouldn't be mad if I got them. But I'm not *expecting* any of them, and I promise you, seeing you smile is more than enough."

"But if you could have more, what would you want?"

His heart kicked up at that and he turned his upper body to her. It was like she had a gravitational pull, coaxing him in bit by bit. He was all caught up in her, looking like a classical beauty, full-figured and sweet. He'd be lying if he denied that his pride swelled as well, knowing that someone who was so dismissive of so many people for some reason found entertainment in his company.

"That's kind of a loaded question," he murmured, trying to study her face for every single movement. He didn't want to misinterpret or assume. Bart had told Benji how he'd almost ruined everything with Missy by taking a kiss she wasn't ready to give him yet.

"I'm a strong woman," she answered smoothly, although red was quickly rising along her face as well. "I can handle a loaded answer."

"Are you sure about that?" he asked, allowing his hand to slide over to hers, his fingertips stroking the top of her fingers.

"Won't know until we find out."

She leaned ever so imperceptibly closer to him, and his hesitation faded enough for him to take the leap. He moved his hand up, letting his fingers trail along the golden skin of her arm, tracing the patterns that her freckles made.

"If I could have more, then the first thing I'd ask for is more dates. I like spending time with you. You make me laugh, and you make me think. Nothing is ever boring with you."

"I think," she drew in a shaking breath as his fingers stopped at the edge of her sleeve, reveling in how soft and pliant her flesh was. "I could be amenable to that."

"Yeah?"

"Yeah."

Another shuddering breath and for some reason it made Benji feel incredibly masculine. The fact that *he* could make her look like *that*, all hazy eyes and enthralled in what he was saying.

"What else?"

"You don't think that's too greedy?"

She shook her head, copper hair bouncing around her face. "No."

"All right."

Another tiny lean closer, his hands trailing up her light shirt, to her shoulder, to her neck, which he gently brushed his fingertips along. It was oh so satisfying to watch goosebumps appear along her skin, proof that maybe she was half as affected by him as he was by her.

"If I could have more, I'd want to hold you. Maybe even never let you go. I've thought about it a lot, you know. Actually, I can't seem to get it out of my head."

To his surprise it was Dani who moved, shifting forward slightly and raising her arms to encircle his neck. Out of nowhere, they were embracing, and Benji wondered if his heart was going to explode right out of his chest.

Their faces were only a few scant inches apart, their breaths mingling with each other as they sat there. It wasn't a starry night full of romance and swoon-worthy lines, but it was Dani in his arms with the pond as her backdrop, looking at him in a way he never thought she would.

"What else?"

Her eyes were half-lidded as she looked up at him, thick lashes shadowing them even further. Goodness, how was she so pretty?

"If I could have more?"

"If you could have more."

He knew there was a chance that he was crossing a line, in fact, his own brother had warned him about it, but Dani was in his arms looking all flushed and wanting and beautiful.

"If I could have more, then I would definitely want to kiss you right now."

She swallowed, and he watched the column of her neck bob.

"If that's what you want, then you should."

He knew an invitation when he heard one, even if it was one that he never expected. Breath hitching, he closed the distance between them and suddenly his mouth was on hers.

It was... so much. Everything. All at once. But at the same time, it wasn't nearly enough. His arms went about her soft waist, his fingers pressing into the give of her. She was so warm, so comforting. He wanted to bury himself in her and never let go.

Her lips moved against his, tentative, but responsive. He could feel her tightening her grip on him, and he took that as encouragement to continue.

And continue he did. He felt like he was on cloud nine, if cloud nine involved him burning up from his feet to his scalp. But man, was it the most pleasurable way to be incinerated that he had ever known.

His hands separated, one gliding up her back to feel her form, coming to rest at the back of her neck. She pressed further into him, aligning the soft femininity of her front with his hardened form, and his fingers gripped her neck harder in response.

She let out a little gasp at that, and the sound caused a reaction in him he never anticipated. Suddenly everything was brighter, sharper, warmer. He was dizzy with how much he wanted her, and how good it felt to be so close. It was easy to get lost in it, and he felt himself ramping up higher and higher.

His other hand went lower, finding the swell of her hip—

Wait.

He pulled himself away suddenly, breathing hard. Dani clearly hadn't been expecting that and nearly toppled forward into him, only held steady by his grip on her.

"What?" she murmured, eyes practically closed, and face thoroughly flushed.

"Sorry," Benji gasped, trying to calm his racing heart.

That had definitely been a rollercoaster ride that he had not prepared for. His body was reacting like he was in a fight, all adrenaline and rushing blood, and he wondered if that was how addicts felt coming down from a high.

"I think, uh, maybe I was getting a bit carried away."

Dani nodded vaguely, pushing herself into a sitting position and looking around. Her lips were kiss-swollen and red, which made him want to repeat the whole process over again.

"Huh. I guess I might have been a bit caught up in it too."

Benji managed to conjure up a very weak laugh. "Well, at least I know it wasn't one-sided."

"No, very much the opposite." She looked up at him with those eyes again, and he could see all the weight behind them settling back in.

He felt good that he had been able to get her to lose at least some of her worries, but they were so quick to return.

"What now?" she asked.

"I'm not sure," Benji admitted honestly. He was still too punch-drunk from that kiss to hide the truth anyway. "But I know that I'd like to see you again, and I'm very serious about dating you."

"Huh," she said, which definitely wasn't an answer at all and made his heart leap in concern. But then she was nodding, as if she was agreeing with a dialogue in her own head. "Yeah. I feel the same. But first..."

"Yeah?" He expected maybe she was going to lay some ground rules or conditions. And that was perfectly fine with him. She could ask him to go get a star for her and he'd find a way to bring one down to Earth.

"How about you take me home in that beautiful buggy?"

"Sure." He swallowed, trying to pull himself away from her. But his hands stayed where they were, wrapped up in all of her and so, *so* warm. "But maybe you should call your parents and tell them we're on our way back."

"Why?" she asked, blinking slowly.

Goodness, they were a pair, weren't they?

"Because then they'll be expecting us, and a little extra responsibility might help me keep my head on straight."

"Benjamin Miller," she said it with mock-dramatics, but the sound of his full name from her still kiss-swollen lips was almost too much. "Are you saying I'm a temptation?"

"I dunno," he responded, letting his fingertips slide along the back of her neck again. "Temptation makes you sound like a negative, and you could never be anything but overwhelmingly positive to me. But yeah, I wouldn't mind kissing you again."

Her face grew so utterly mischievous that he knew he was gonna be in trouble. "Then do it."

"Dani, you're going to be the death of me," he said with a laugh, going instead to kiss the tip of her nose. His body was still thrumming with desire for her, and he knew he needed to cut himself off while he could.

"Yeah, but what a way to go."

20

———

Danielle

"You look happy today," Mom said, sipping at her coffee while Dani practically floated through the kitchen.

"I am happy," Dani answered breezily.

Still cautious, but also happy. Relaxed. It seemed that Keiko was right, lowering her walls did allow someone wonderful to slip in.

It'd been two days since the surprise date in the buggy, and just like the perfect gentleman, Benji had taken her home and given her a chaste kiss on the lips on her porch.

Everything had happened so fast that day, she'd never had time to tell him that he was her first kiss. That she'd never felt close or safe enough with anyone to try something like that. But the moment his lips had touched hers, thoughts of anybody else flew out of her head and there was only him.

And *boy,* was he something.

Dani had always scoffed at books and movies that focused on kisses like they could change the world. It was just one human pushing their mouth bits up against another human's mouth bits and getting all carbon dioxide with each other. But goodness, she was of a very different opinion now. While yeah, maybe the world hadn't suddenly shifted on its axis, it felt like *her* world had, and she was choosing to enjoy it rather than overthink it.

Which was only slightly difficult.

That voice inside of her told her that it couldn't last. That it was a trick. That she was being dumb. But she shoved that down, *down*, *down*, until it was just a faint whisper behind all the pleasantness.

"I'm glad. We were a little bit worried about you, you know."

There was that sliver of guilt again. But this time she let herself feel it, process it, and move on. No more ruminating and overthinking about every negative thing that passed through her mind.

"I'm sorry. I've had a lot going on in my head, and I feel like I'm just beginning to straighten it out."

"I see," she answered, sipping more of her coffee. "And is that Miller boy the one that's doing all the straightening?"

Dani felt herself turn red, but her mother just laughed and continued talking.

"I like him. He's a sweet boy. We wouldn't be remotely where we are now if it weren't for him and his family."

"No, we definitely would not," Dani agreed.

"But you're not doing this because you feel like you owe him something, right? Because charity is something that's freely given, not used as a bargaining chip later."

"Oh no, Mom. It's nothing like that. I promise. He's a good guy. I guess we're kind of seeing where things are going."

She didn't tell her mother about the investment Benji was considering. That felt like it would be violating his trust.

"I thought as much," her mom said, rising and crossing to press a kiss to Dani's cheek. "My girl has always been too strong for things like that. I'm so blessed to have a daughter that takes after the likeness of me."

"Oh, so *you're* the one who gave me my temper and propensity for conflict?"

She snorted as she put her empty mug in the sink and for a moment it really was like looking in a mirror. "Back in my day, we called it having a backbone. The world is all too happy to crush people like us, Dani. I'll always be grateful that you seem to know how to push it right back."

The words were surprisingly sweet. Not because her mother wasn't always loving and verbal about that love, but because her mom certainly seemed to know what to say and exactly when to say it.

"Thanks, Mom."

"Of course, dear. Your father and I are about to head to the city to sign what will hopefully be the last of the insurance papers and visit your brothers. Do you need anything?"

Dani shook her head. Everything she wanted was already around. What a wild thought.

"All right. Be good. Try not to work yourself too hard. And, oh, I realize now that I've never had to say this to you, but I remember what it was like to be young and in love. If you end up alone with that Miller boy, make—"

"*Mom*," Dani cut her off sternly. "I am twenty-six years old. If you are about to give me a birds and the bees or be careful talk, the need for that has *long* since passed."

"All right, fine, fine. Fair enough. But you are my youngest one. Can you blame me for wanting to protect you?" She reached up to gently caress Dani's cheek. "My little girl, but so much a woman."

Dani pressed her face into her mother's touch, eyes fluttering closed. Ever since the fire with her brothers, she realized that she'd been holding her parents at bay too. Not wanting to inconvenience them or burden them when everything was her fault anyway. But now it didn't feel as selfish to lean on them a little.

"I love you, Mom."

"I love you too, dear."

They parted a bit after, both of them going about their day, but Dani made sure to run to the end of the garden and wave to them as they pulled down the drive and headed toward the dirt road that would eventually lead them to the highway.

After that, it was just a matter of busying herself with the chores that three siblings used to do all together. It wasn't that bad, however, because she knew Benji would eventually show up and cover a lot of the ones her brothers used to do. Sure, she'd rather have her own siblings on it considering the reason why they weren't around, but he wasn't a bad substitute in a pinch.

As if he had heard her thoughts, she was in the middle of refilling her canteen with cold water when there was a knock at the back door. She looked out the window to see Benji standing there, looking handsome and casual in his work clothes, so she motioned him in.

"Hey there," she said, nerves and excitement bubbling up in her middle. It was strange to be so honest about her feelings when she normally spent so much time denying them, but not entirely unwelcome. "Did you need something?"

"Need? No. Want? Yes."

He took a couple strides toward her and placed a kiss on the top of her head. Perhaps it all was a bit too fast, going from never having been kissed to suddenly having someone in front of her who was clearly willing to show his affection, but she liked the change. It made her feel wanted in a way she never had before.

While she'd really never needed a relationship to feel whole, or for any sort of fulfillment, she realized it was nice to have someone outside of her family to lean on. It made her feel less isolated. More accepted.

More willing to trust.

"How about lunch?" she asked, her body heating up just by his close proximity.

She had never expected to have such a visceral reaction to him, but even just the smell of him reminded her of that amazing kiss and how it had practically made her head spin.

"Sure," he said with a soft smile. "Lunch sounds nice."

Dani nodded and slipped away from him, going to the fridge to make them a couple of cold cut sandwiches. Nothing fancy, of course, but it was filling and cool, which was nice on a warm summer day.

"You a ham or a turkey kind of guy?" she asked, happy to have something to take her mind off the many distracting details about him.

"How about both?"

"Both?" she echoed. "What is this madness?"

"I'm a growing boy. I like my protein."

"I'll say so. Condiments?"

"You got spicy mustard?"

"Do I have spicy mustard?" she asked sarcastically. "Does the pope wear a funny hat?"

She grabbed the three different types of heated mustard they had and tossed them over to Benji, who caught each one of them.

"Huh, I don't think we even have this many at our house."

"Well, we've got eclectic tastes here in the house of Touhey. Believe it or not, I don't even like mustard. Those just belong to my brothers and Ma."

"You don't like mustard?" he asked incredulously. "Huh, I guess there was a reason nobody liked you in high school after all."

Her jaw dropped at the joke, and she tossed the entire loaf of bread at him.

"Excuse me, how *dare* you relate my very serious trauma to a sandwich topping."

"What? It all makes sense now. Who *doesn't* like mustard? They must have sensed that something was wrong."

Despite the dark subject, the joking made her laugh, and she felt her spirits lifting even higher as she went about making their sandwiches. When she sat next to him, handing him his plate, she ruffled his hair.

It was uncanny how easily the physical affection came to her. Like the only reason she had been so stressed lately was because she had kept herself so bottled up in her own head. Leave it to Keiko to have everything all figured out and find a solution.

Benji practically inhaled the sandwich as soon as she set it down, draining the glass as well. She gave him a keen sort of look, then quickly made him another one. She liked being a good host almost as much as she liked seeing him enthusiastically eat what she made. Normally, she would have to worry about the grocery budget and if it was really worth it before having a second helping, but considering all the help his family had given them, she knew her fridge was going to be stocked for a good, long time.

"What?" Benji asked, realizing that she was staring at him.

"Just thinking," she said happily, taking his plate and carrying it over to the sink. She turned on the faucet only to feel his strong form pressed against her back, and then his hands were parting her hair so he could gently kiss at the nape of her neck.

"You know, when I woke up this morning, I was almost afraid that I had dreamed it all."

She stood there a moment, goosebumps rising along her arms as she let herself enjoy his affection, but eventually she turned around, so their fronts were pressed together.

He was a lot taller than her, so even standing on her tip toes, she had to strain her neck upward. He caught her intent right away though, and soon his lips were crashing to hers once more.

It was so... *nice.* Being wanted. Being loved. Having someone there to comfort her. Perhaps it was silly to stake so much on a kiss, but she couldn't help how much it eased the ache inside of her. No, it didn't erase the fact that her brothers were in the hospital, or that she had other things to work through. But it did make those things so much easier to bear.

Benji pressed into her, kissing her lips tenderly yet passionately. That made her knees weak, but he seemed to anticipate that, as his arms squeezed tighter around her.

Briefly she wondered if she should stop him, if they were going too far too fast and going to get themselves into something they weren't ready for. But then he was hauling her up, setting her down on the counter so she was more level with him, and he didn't have to stoop to kiss her.

Dani would like to say that she handled it smoothly, but she let out a surprised little squeak. She knew that Benji was strong because of ranch life, but she had no idea he was *that* strong. She wasn't exactly a sack of flour.

She was more like a bushel or two.

But Benji just chuckled, pulling away from her slightly to rest his forehead against hers. "Is this all right?" he asked.

His voice sounded absolutely *wrecked*. Something about the raggedness made her feel somewhat vain, preening at the fact that *she* was doing that to him.

"Maybe we should breathe for a moment," she murmured, laughing a bit awkwardly too.

"Yeah, breathing is important, last I heard."

"Really? Sounds like fake news."

"You know what, you're right. Guess you should just kiss me again."

She leaned toward him, definitely ready to fall into the syrupy headiness of his affection, but then her phone rang, nearly jolting her from the moment.

"I sure hope you're planning on ignoring that," Benji said ruefully as she pulled her cellphone from the front of her overalls.

"Only about seven people have my number. None of them are people I'd ignore."

"Huh, I guess one of us has to be responsible."

"Responsible, yeah."

She finally got her phone out and looked at the screen. It was her Ma, and instantly her stomach dropped out of her body and down towards China. She knew that it was probably just her calling in to say they were going to end up spending the night in a motel, but she felt herself automatically defaulting to the worst assumptions.

"Hey, Ma, what's up?"

"Honey, are you home?"

Dani could instantly tell that something was wrong with her mom's tone. She put her hand on Benji's muscled chest to push him away, hopping to the ground as he instantly moved for her.

"Yeah, Mom. You okay?"

"Yes, honey. But is Benji there?"

Her cheeks burned a bit. "Yeah. Why?"

"Okay Dani, stay calm for me, please?"

Her whole body went cold at that. "*Mom*, what's happening?"

"They're going to try to wake up James. We asked them to wait for you, but they say the doctor only has about an hour and a half. Can Benji get you here? I want you to be here if he wakes up. I know he's going to ask for you."

"What about Chester?" she asked, heart pounding in her chest. They were waking her brother up. After weeks of waiting, worrying, she was finally going to be able to talk to her brother and apologize for ever putting him into that mess.

"His vitals haven't been as steady as James so they want to wait a couple more days. Do you think you can come, honey?"

Dani looked to Benji, who was watching her with a concerned expression. "They're gonna wake my brother up," she managed to say, which seemed almost impossible considering that her mouth felt like sandpaper.

His eyebrows shot up and he stood straight. "Really?"

She could only nod, her mouth giving up on that whole talking thing.

"Then let's go!"

Her heart squeezed gratefully, and she spoke into the phone again, forcing the words out. "Yeah, Mom. I'll be there as soon as I can."

"Thank you, honey. I think I need you here too. Just in... just in case."

"Of course, Mom. We're leaving now."

"Love you, Dani."

"Love you too."

The screen door punctuated her statement, slamming closed as she and Benji hurried toward his truck. He had parked it where he usually did, and within minutes they were jumping inside and flying down the drive.

"You okay?" Benji asked, looking at her out of the corner of his eye while he drove.

Dani just nodded, focusing her eyes ahead as if she could get them to the hospital faster by doing so. She knew the risks of waking her brother up. The foremost being that he wouldn't *actually* wake up. But there were other things too. That the influx of pain would put him into shock even with all the medicine he was taking, that his immune system could tank. She just had to hope that wouldn't happen.

She had to hope for the best.

After all, hoping for the best with Benji had worked out all right. Maybe this would too.

21

———

Danielle

$\mathcal{D}$ani's leg bounced as they reached the edge of the city, traffic slowing them down considerably. They'd been making such good time. She hated the thought that a red light or a person who didn't know how to merge properly on the highway could make her miss her reunion with her brother.

"It's gonna be okay," Benji soothed, keeping his gaze on the road as he tried to circumvent the delays as best he could.

"I'm trying not to think of how it's *going* to be," Dani admitted, her leg bouncing harder. "I'm just trying to focus on getting there."

"That's not a bad idea. One thing at a time, right?"

She nodded, throat tight. Her Ma was texting her on and off, giving her progress reports and the like. They apparently had started easing a lot of the meds her brother was on since that morning, but they wouldn't do the final step until she was there.

Or an hour and a half passed. Whichever came first.

Thankfully, the hospital came into sight when they still had twenty minutes to spare. Dani quickly tried to mentally calculate how long it would take Benji to park and then walk up to the elevators and then finally get to her brothers' room.

"I'm going to drop you off at the side entrance. That's the one you said is closest to your brothers, right?"

"You remember that?" Dani asked. She might have mentioned that once, but she wasn't even sure.

"Yeah. I made a point to keep it in mind in case I ever drove you to visit your brothers."

"Wow, that is really sweet, but I don't have time to give you a proper thanks because I'm too busy thinking about how fast I can vault out of your truck and up to the room."

"That's fine," he said with a grin. "You've got more important things to worry about. Just don't break a leg, okay."

"I'll try not to. I want to visit my brothers in the hospital. Not be admitted."

"Good. Remember that."

He finally pulled up to the entrance, and she popped her seatbelt off and jumped out. As soon as her feet hit the ground, she was off and power walking to the elevators.

She knew to text her mom that she was on the way up before she got into those metal boxes because she would lose all signal. She didn't get her mother's response in time, but that didn't matter.

She was going to make it.

That thought had her bouncing from foot to foot in the elevator, eyes locked on the lights that indicated what floor she was on. 1... 2... 3... it seemed to take forever, and she wondered how effectively medical personnel could get around with elevators that took a literal age of man to get where they needed to go.

She managed to survive until the doors opened then rushed to her brother's room. The path was familiar despite her only being there a handful of times, but it took on a whole new feeling as she rushed to her destination.

"Dani!"

It was Mom who noticed her first, getting to her feet and throwing her arms around her daughter in a hug. Dani clung to her as well, nodding to her dad who stepped out of the room. She assumed to tell a nurse that she was finally there.

"Where's Benji?" Mom asked when she stepped away from her.

"He went to park the car. He wanted to make sure that I didn't miss this."

"That's real considerate of him."

"Yeah. He seems to be so far."

"Look at you," Mom said, her hands gently squeezing Dani's arms. "Opening up and trusting people. I'm so proud of you dear."

Dani felt herself blush. "Aw, it ain't a big deal, Mom."

"To me it is."

Dani wasn't about to argue and settled for waiting for the doctor. It turned out that Benji had been very smart indeed, because the doctor, an older woman with silver hair pulled back in a tight bun, came in before he could make it back from the parking lot.

"Ah, are we ready?" she asked, her voice sounding perfectly neutral.

"Yes, please," Mom murmured, her fingers intertwining with Dani's.

There was a lot of moving about, with two nurses coming into the room. One of them stated they were going to turn down his sedation medication.

"What now?" Dani found herself asking, looking to the doctor with what she hoped was a steady gaze.

"Now you wait. He can take anywhere from five minutes to five hours to wake up. Or he could not wake up at all, and we will address that *if* that happens, although it seems unlikely at this juncture."

"Okay, thank you."

"Of course. I'll have my nurses stay here and monitor things. They'll page me if anything is amiss, but we're anticipating a smooth transition. Do you have any questions?"

"No," Dad said, his voice a low rumble.

Anyone who didn't know him wouldn't catch the tremor in his words, but Dani did. Poor Dad. If there was anyone that she had gotten her tendency to bottle things up from, it was him.

"All right then. I'll see you back in here soon."

The doctor stepped out and then that was that.

But Dani wasn't content to just stand there, staring at her brother, so she busied herself with pushing all of the chairs in the room closer to his bed, with one of them being close enough to his left side so that someone could hold his hand.

And that someone was Mom, of course. Dani gestured for her to take a seat and thankfully, she did without protest. It was harder to get her dad to sit next to her, the man seeming to want to pace around rather than wait. But if James woke up, she didn't want him seeing his father walking back and forth hurriedly—something the man only did when he was very upset.

No, she wanted her brother to wake up with loving faces all around him and kind smiles.

Finally, she sat on his right side. She couldn't hold his hands or stroke his arm because of his burns, but she could gently pet his head. Which she did, murmuring about how she was so excited to see him again and that he was definitely going to need to dust his room once he was back home.

Minutes passed, and little by little, she noticed signs of life coming to her brother. At first, it was just a slight twitch in the muscles of his face. Then it was his tongue coming out to try to wet his lips, which were so cracked and dry. Apparently, the nurses came and applied balm and wetted down his mouth several times each rotation, but it wasn't enough to stop them from becoming dehydrated with his breathing tube in place.

But each little sign was like a blessing, and she felt hope rising higher and higher in her chest as she categorized them all.

A knock on the door drew her attention for a moment and she saw Benji standing there, looking breathless.

"Hey," he said softly. "Do you want me to wait out here?"

"No, no," Dani said quickly, gesturing for him to come in. "It's all right."

Benji gave an uncertain look to her parents, but they nodded too. Quickly, he strolled over to Dani, his large hand resting on her shoulder.

While before his touch had lit a fire in her, making her burn with all sorts of wants that decent people weren't supposed to have, now it soothed her. Made her feel safe. Supported. She didn't have enough brain power left over to analyze that, so she just let herself accept the good feelings.

To their credit, the nurses stayed quiet as they came in and out of the room, never leaving for more than a few minutes and one of them always within earshot.

It was an hour and forty-five minutes later that her brother's eyes first fluttered open, flying wide in confusion. Dani was instantly leaning over him, talking low and smooth.

"Hey there. You're in the hospital. You're safe, okay? We're right here with you."

She could see his pupils dilate as his eyes roved around, trying to place everything. She didn't know how much he was aware of when he was in his coma, so she just let him do what he needed, staying alert in case he hurt himself.

The tension lasted for a few minutes, but he seemed to simmer when he saw Mom and Dad along with her. Blinking slowly, he tried to raise his head but then his breathing tube let out a horrible gagging sound.

"Uh, nurse—"

But one of the women was already in the room with a towel and suction equipment in her hands. "It looks like someone is ready to have their breathing tube pulled out. Would you mind making space?"

Naturally, it was Dani who moved first, then the RN and the respiratory therapist came up alongside James, going about their business quickly and efficiently with smiles on their faces.

"All right, we're going to take your breathing tube out. Sound good?" Her brother slowly nodded his head yes. "We just have to take this tape off, then we'll pull it out, and we want you to give us a few big coughs once it's out, okay?"

Her brother blinked slowly again, and the respiratory therapist took that as affirmation. With the ease that could only come from years of experience, she pulled the tube out, holding the towel under James' chin to catch the drool, mucus and what looked like soot that came out with it.

Her brother coughed once, twice, three times before letting out a strangled groan. It made Dani's heart shatter, but the nurse reacted as patient and smoothly as ever, crossing to the bathroom and wetting a cloth before returning to James and gently wetting down his mouth.

"There," she said soothingly, and Dani was a bit in awe of her. "Feel better?"

He winced a little, a small rasp coming from his throat. She nodded like she understood.

"Are you in pain?"

Another little rasp.

"All right. I'll go get the doctor and see what we can give you for that. In the meantime, I want you to breathe for me, okay? Long, slow, and deep as you can. You're doing great, James."

She looked to the family with a small nod before heading out the door. "He's looking good. I know it all looked a little scary, but he's doing just fine. Don't worry." And then she was gone.

As time passed, her brother seemed to grow more lucid, his sluggish gazes turning sharper and like the sibling Dani remembered. He didn't talk, only little choking sounds and wheezes coming from his dry throat, but he found ways to communicate anyway.

It was Mom who told him everything that happened. From the ambulance ride to his induced coma and all the treatments he had been getting. How debriding his skin had taken two plastic surgeons hours and hours even with the two of them and how he was going to need skin grafts in the future.

It was scary stuff, but she also told him how he never got a single infection and how the doctors were impressed with his recovery. She told him about the insurance and how the town had really rallied around them.

She told him about almost everything and anything, continuing as the doctor came in and gave James something that seemed to help him settle, and not stopping until everything was out.

Well, everything except what was going on with Dani and Benji, that wasn't hers to tell.

By the end of it all, the sun had set in the sky and James was leaning back in his pillows, a slight grin on his face. He looked thoroughly exhausted though, and Dad asked him if he wanted to rest.

He tapped his left pointer finger twice against Mom's hand, his signal for a yes. Mom asked if he wanted them to stay, and that was another yes.

Unfortunately, hospital rules were only one person was supposed to be allowed to spend the night, so that meant Dani was out. The only reason Dad would be able to stay along with Mom was because Chester shared the same room as Benji and technically that fit the rules of one overnight guest per person.

Bending down to press the gentlest kiss she could on her brother's head, Dani wished him goodnight before crossing over to Chester. She gave him a kiss too and assured him that his time was coming, he just had to keep fighting.

With one last hug for the night to her Mom and Dad, she headed out of the room, Benji following silently behind her.

They stayed silent all the way to the car, her mind so full she felt like she might burst.

She was just so, *so* happy. She knew that this was just the beginning, that he had a lot of work to do going forward and there could be all sorts of speedbumps along the way. But she couldn't help but be relieved that she was getting her big brother back.

Thank God.

But also, she couldn't help but wish that he could have stayed awake a bit longer so she could tell him about Benji and maybe ask him for some advice. But that would mean shooing everyone out of his room so there probably wouldn't have been a good time for that.

It wasn't until they pulled out of the parking lot and onto the street when she felt she finally had her wits about her enough to speak.

"Thank you," she said, looking at Benji gratefully.

"No problem. I'm happy I was able to be there for you."

"Yeah, you really were, weren't you?" She breathed in through her nose and out through her mouth. "I know I would have been able to survive all of this without you, but goodness, I'm real happy that you were here."

He smiled at that, and they drove in silence for a while. But once they got more onto the country roads, he began to shift around a little.

"You okay over there?" she asked, eyeing him.

"Yeah, it's just..." He took a deep breath and for a moment she was sure that he was about to tell her that she was all too much and so was her family. "I know this is probably fast, but I don't want to just casually go on dates and make out in your kitchen."

Crap.

She knew this would happen. Her heart broke and it took everything in her not to let her eyes get teary. Just when things were starting to go well, something always came around to bite her.

"I realized in that hospital room how easy it is for someone to be snatched away, so I don't want to waste any time playing around. I want a relationship. Maybe it's juvenile, but I want to introduce you as my girlfriend, not just a woman I happen to be dating."

"Oh."

"Oh?"

"Very *oh*."

"I gotta admit, when you ask a beautiful woman if she's interested in something serious, you usually hope to hear something a little more... affirmative."

"Right. *Right.* I just, whew, I thought you were trying to end everything with me."

He actually took his eyes off the road, staring at her. "What? Why would I do that?"

"I dunno. Still expecting the worse, I guess. Working on that."

He reached over and squeezed her hand.

"It's okay. I understand that past experiences have definitely made a pattern. But trust me, I'm like a barnacle. You're gonna have to pry me off with some sort of sharp instrument."

"Huh, you know that sounds like torture."

"Uh, please don't torture me."

"I'll try not to."

Their banter faded into light laughter and he looked back to the road, but she could still feel the corner of his gaze on her.

"So, is that a yes?"

Dani smiled, warmth and happiness bubbling through her. "Well, I'm tempted."

"Oh, you're tempted, huh?"

"I just might be."

"I guess sometimes temptation isn't a bad thing."

"Not from where I'm sitting. So yeah, that's a yes."

The road was empty, so he leaned over, giving her a light kiss. Dani pushed into it for a moment, before forcing herself to behave. After all, she wouldn't be a good girlfriend if the two of them ended up smeared across the road.

Ew. Dark thoughts. The situation with her brothers had given her a definite macabre edge to her dry humor.

Oh well. It was something she could work on. Because after her little experiment, she could honestly say that she was ready to trust someone again.

Maybe... even ready to love.

But she didn't want to get ahead of herself, not when she was on a journey with someone who mattered so much to her. She was going to value every step along the way. The stumbles, the bumbles, and the victories.

Life was finally looking up, and she was going to enjoy it.

One kiss at a time.

EPILOGUE

A year and a half later

Benji

"Are you sure you're all right?" Dani asked for maybe the tenth time since he had picked her up. She was staring at him with that too-knowing gaze of hers, and he knew she was zooming in on each and every little sign that he might be giving off.

"I'm just not really much for parties, and this is the first one we've had with *everyone* there. And I mean everyone. Even our cousins from Dakota have flown in."

She reached across the seat and patted his hand, her skin as soft as ever. "I think it's real amazing that your whole family is getting together just to have a cookout and reconnect. And that you invited my whole family, of course."

"Why would I ever want to go to any sort of celebration if you weren't there?" he retorted back, looking in his rearview mirror to double-check that both sets of parents were following behind them.

It'd been a year and a half since that fateful ride back to her home from the hospital, and Benji had cherished every moment of it. The journey wasn't easy, with plenty of people disrespecting Dani when he wasn't around, or starting up the rumor mill, but between him, his brothers, Ma, Pa, Chastity, Missy, and Keiko, Dani now had one heck of a backup system. Eventually, people's attitudes started to change about her, and Benji was pleased when he heard that Rachel had decided to move to the Big Apple after being fired from the diner.

Not that he would ever want to chase someone out of town, but that woman wasn't exactly adding to the environment. She was mean, vicious and he was glad that her shadow no longer would cross any of their paths.

Thankfully, the arsonists had been caught and secured in the juvenile detention center. They had a history of vandalism and started the fires for excitement, not for revenge or because they were targeting anyone specifically. When they heard about the extensive burns the Touhey brothers suffered, the teens were truly sorry.

Her brothers had done incredibly well for themselves, with Chester being brought out of his coma just a week after James. From there they'd spent six months in the burn unit with their first couple of skin grafts, and then there was a whole lot of physical therapy.

It wasn't until the eleventh month that they were allowed home, and they still had a twenty-four-hour nurse on hand for all the little things they needed assistance with. Benji had been able to tell that it sometimes grated on their nerves, so he'd started taking them on short fishing jaunts or walks around his ranch. He hadn't expected it to happen, but the three of them formed a bond so fast that they quickly became his best friends.

It was odd, perhaps, to be so integrated into the Touhey family, but that was exactly how he felt. He went over there at least every other day even though all the damage from the fire was long gone, and his own brothers had grown used to his absence. Of course, Dani always pestered him about getting his work done on his own family's ranch, but he would just make excuses that he wanted to check on his investment.

Because, after a whole lot of research by Bradley, he had ended up working something out investing in the Touhey's goat enterprise. He wasn't a co-owner or anything like that, but it was enough to help diversify his portfolio and support something that he thoroughly believed in.

All in all, he couldn't have asked for a better eighteen months.

"You *sure* you're all right?" Dani asked again, reaching up to poke his cheek. "You've got your thinking face on."

"What's wrong with thinking?" he shot back.

That was his girl all right. After all their time together, she'd learned to read his face like a book. There was no point in ever trying to keep anything from her; she could almost always tell at a glance when he was plotting.

Not that he needed to keep secrets from her. He believed in communication, and given Dani's depression, there were hundreds of times that they had to talk things out to get on the same page. It was just that... well, sometimes it was nice to have a trick up his sleeve.

Or in his pocket.

He swallowed *hard* at that, forcing his thoughts away lest she read his mind like the mythical creature she was.

"Nothing's wrong with it, per se. But it's weird that you have that face when we're just going to a party. Who *thinks* at a barbeque? You're just supposed to eat too much and make generic small talk with relatives you won't see for several years."

"What can I say? I got a lot on my mind."

"Like what?"

"Like how I got so lucky to end up with a beauty like you on my arm. I'm gonna have to fight off my cousins with a stick."

She blushed at that, quickly changing the subject as she looked out of the window. Just as he had hoped. Even after all of their time together, she still would flush and sputter when he complimented her. Her brothers all warned that he was going to give her the biggest head, but he didn't care. If he could remind her every moment that she was magnificent, he would. Anything to counteract that dark, mean voice inside of her she told him about.

And it wasn't like he was giving her empty compliments. She was absolutely stunning every day, but when she got extra special dressed up for him, she was just *impossibly beautiful.*

He glanced at her again out of the corner of his eye. She was wearing a pale, lilac dress made out of several layers of chiffon. It floated gently around her figure, and she wore a pair of old-fashioned thigh highs with the line up the back.

He forced his mind away from the image of her thick thighs in them and drifted over the rest of her. Her copper hair was done up in victory rolls and she had a classic face of makeup on. Little pink sunglasses completed her look, reminding him of a classic pinup girl, but so much more.

How was it that even after all of this time, he was as intensely attracted to her as he had been from the start? He didn't know, but he certainly wasn't complaining. The only time it was an issue was when they were alone and the soft beauty of her body grew into too heady of a temptation.

"Why are your cheeks pink?"

"No reason," he replied quickly, forcing his eyes back on the road.

But she shifted in her seat beside him, crossing her legs and her fingers snapping something several times. It took him several seconds to realize that she was playing with one of the straps of her garters, making it hit her thigh repeatedly to make the dramatic sound.

"You're evil, you know that?" he accused.

"I'm just trying to distract you," she said innocently, fluttering her lashes at him.

If there was one thing he had learned in his year and a half with his girlfriend, it was that she loved to tease him whenever she could.

"So you won't be nervous about your family."

"You truly are a martyr."

"Anything for the man I love."

His heart thumped at that. Another thing he didn't think he'd ever get used to. She *loved* him.

Him.

Not Ben, the eldest and largest inheritor of the Miller dynasty. Not Bart and all of his muscles and glory. Not Bradley and his genius. She loved *Benjamin Miller* and *Benjamin Miller* only.

What a world.

They arrived at the ranch before he could get too overwhelmed with that thought, Ben pulling up with Dani's parents and her brothers driving the family truck. They all parked without much difficulty considering the fleet of cars that were sitting there and headed toward the main house.

From there things started to pick up, with the women of the family helping Ma load things out onto the tables under the massive tent they had set up outside while the men proceeded to start up the grills. Normally, such a stark gender separation would never happen at a Miller event considering the broad range of personalities and interests, but he had enlisted his family in making sure they kept Dani occupied.

"Hey there, little brother," Bart said from where he was working the large, open grill that Grandpa Miller had made. "You look nauseous."

"I *feel* nauseous. What if she hates this?"

"She won't," he said with a solid nod. "That girl had issues with being an outcast in the past, right? Nothing will make an impact on her more than making a statement in front of every single family member you can."

"Right. Right. I mean, it's no dinner at a fancy Italian restaurant."

"Hey, that was for my lady. This is for yours. That's like expecting Missy's wedding to be the same as Chastity's was."

Benji snorted at that. "I don't think I could imagine two women with more different styles than those two."

"Right?" Bart laughed. "Sometimes I see Chastity helping Missy with planning our wedding, and Chastity has this look on her face like she's trying not to get a headache from all the pastels."

"Missy sure does love those pastels," Benji agreed with a nod.

When he first found out about her preferred wedding colors, he'd been surprised. For a woman with muscles that rivaled his and a scowl that could intimidate a coyote, she apparently went cuckoo for anything having to do with unicorns and pretty, soft colors.

"That she does. And I love her. Anyway, enough about me. Are you ready for this? There's no going back."

"Yeah, I'm well aware."

"Funny how we all kind of found a lady in order, isn't it?"

"Uncanny, maybe." Benji sighed and his hand went to his pocket, the weight there grounding him to the moment. "Say, is there anything that needs to be done that involves a lot of heavy lifting and not much brain?"

"Hah! Yeah, I think Pa is cutting wood in the back. I'm sure he wouldn't mind a hand."

"Great."

Benji gave his brother a nod and then headed around the house. Sure enough, Pa was there, chopping wood like any sixty-seven-year-old was wont to do. Benji mostly just ended up hauling it around to the grills and fire pit out front, but at least it got his mind off things.

By the time he was all done, everyone was out, about and mingling. He caught up with Dani and Keiko, who were both smiling and sipping some punch. Then his mother was saying a prayer and everyone was lining up for grub.

It really was some impressive spread, enough to feed the hundred some-odd Millers and cousins that were present. Benji was pretty sure that even their adopted family from the east was there, descended from someone generations ago that he didn't quite remember the story of.

Something about a train robbery and a mute? He'd have to ask his Ma later.

There were ribs, and brisket that had been cooking since the previous day. Collard greens, ham, corn on the cob, potato salad. Salmon, kebabs, all sorts of squash. It was better than Thanksgiving, although that also was partially due to the massive platter of wings that they had ordered from Chester's favorite wing place in the city.

Benji had dropped a very pretty penny on the gathering, but it was worth it. Or at least, it would be if it all turned out how he wanted.

He filled his plate even though his stomach was churning, nerves simmering just under his skin. Somehow Dani managed not to notice it, but that was probably because she was staring at all of the food in wonder.

It was cute that she never seemed to get used to the wealth and all the things that he took for granted. It made him appreciate things more, never letting him forget that it would be so easy to have nothing.

He led her to a table in the center, right where he planned it, and soon they were all digging in.

There was lots of good conversations and jokes, but Benji was only half paying attention. His mind was ahead of himself, waiting until before the desserts were brought out.

It was with a glance to his brothers, who gave him a nod, and then he stood up.

"Benji, what are you doing?" Dani asked, looking up at him in confusion as he clinked his fork against his mug.

But he just winked at her, taking her hand in his and pulling her to her feet. She stood, flushing as she realized all eyes were on them.

"Uh, Benji?"

Well, he could tease too. He stood there for a moment, staring at that beautiful face, before he finally sank to one knee.

The response was instantaneous, cheers rose up from everyone around them while Dani's hand went to cover the shocked gasp that escaped her mouth.

"Benji..." she whispered, eyes so wide that he would have chuckled if it were any other moment.

"Danielle Touhey," he started, trying to keep his voice steady. "You have made the past year and a half of my life more amazing than I ever thought possible. I wake up every morning happy to see you, and I go to bed at night happy to dream of you. You've helped me grow as a person. To be better, kinder, and more appreciative of everything I have.

"And I want to share all that I have with you. Because you make everything more. Better. I want our entire future to be bound up together until I forget what it was ever like to be lonely."

Goodness, his heart was thundering, and his mouth was going dry, but he pressed onward. Dani was crying now, eyes watering as she looked down at him.

Still holding her hand, he reached into his pocket with his free one. Opening the little box he pulled out, he held up the ring to her.

It was a simple band, but one that was completely her. Made of platinum, there was only a single stone in the center, and it was an emerald just like her mother's. It was the birth month that they shared, and she had always told him she didn't get the hype about diamonds.

"Dani, would you do me the honor of being my wife?"

"Oh my *gosh,* yes, Benji. *Yes!*"

He slid the ring onto her finger, and she practically hauled him up by his collar. He barely managed to steady himself before she threw her arms around his shoulders and crashed her lips to his.

It was just as dizzying as it had ever been, and he gripped her just as eagerly. His heart soared and he couldn't believe it, even as more whoops and hollers sounded from all around them.

When they finally did part, he was breathless again and so was Dani, looking up at him as tears streamed down her face. The pure joy in her eyes made her radiant, and he wanted to bask in the glow of her for the rest of his life.

And she'd said yes, so there was a pretty high chance of that actually happening.

Giddy with it all, he bent down and gave her another short kiss before everyone closed in on them. Soon the couple was inundated with screams and hugs and congratulations, but Benji refused to let any of the well-wishers separate them.

Eventually, things started to settle again and Benji looked over the massive crowd with the love of his life by his side. A lot had changed since they'd met, including him, but he knew without a doubt, he was no longer the forgotten middle child he'd thought he was.

No, he was Benjamin Miller, soon-to-be husband of Danielle Touhey, the strongest, most beautiful woman he knew.

What kind of better fate could he ask for?

~

HELLO READER... I hope you enjoyed Her Rival Cowboy. The next sweet romance up in Brothers of Miller Ranch is Her Fake-Fiance Cowboy Protector. It's not just any fake-fiance romance. True to this series, it tackles deeper issues and of course has an amazingly handsome and humble Miller brother in it.

With an average rating of 4.6 stars, readers love this book just as much as they loved the first three. One reader had this to say: "This is beautifully written. Seeing the entire Miller family gather around and support Sophia. An all around great read."

You can find Bradley and Sophia's story on all major retailers. Plus, you can find it on my own online bookstore if you'd like to support my small mom-owned business. I'd be honored if you chose to do so. Scan the QR code below to be taken to Her Fake-Fiance Cowboy Protector at Natalie Dean Books. If scanning QR codes isn't your thing, you can also find my store here: nataliedeanbooks.com

Born and raised in a small coastal town in the south, I was raised to treasure family and love the Lord. I'm a dedicated homeschooling mom who loves to travel and spend time with my growing-up-too-fast son.

When I'm not busy writing or running my business, you can find me cleaning house, cooking dinner, feeding our three rescue cats, trying to make learning fun and coaxing my son to pick up his toys. On less busy days, you may also find me paddling down a spring run in Florida, hiking a mountain trail in Georgia (on the rare vacation to the mountains), or enjoying a book.

If you love Natalie Dean books, you can be notified of new releases by signing up to my newsletter at nataliedeanauthor.com, where you will also receive two free short stories for signing up. Just click on the "Free Books" tab at the top and you'll be on your way!

Also, as previously mentioned, I've opened my own online bookstore and I'd love your support! As of June 2024, I'm selling my ebooks at Natalie Dean Books. By late summer or fall 2024, I should have audiobooks, regular paperbacks, large print paperbacks, dyslexic print paperbacks and signed paperbacks all available. At the request of my loyal readers, I'll also be adding merchandise, such as glasses, cups, magnets and more. So come check out my small mom-owned author business at nataliedeanbooks.com.

You can also scan the QR code below to be taken to the home page of Natalie Dean Books.

facebook.com/nataliedeanromance

www.ingramcontent.com/pod-product-compliance
Lightning Source LLC
Chambersburg PA
CBHW032303310726
48973CB00008B/2509